UNSAVORY COMPANY

KATE PAVELLE

Mugen Press
Pittsburgh, PA

This book is dedicated to my parents
who took me places as a kid
like abroad
as refugees
bumming around Europe as a teen
not speaking the languages
learning to survive for just another day
shelter that sprouting seed
so later, when the sun comes out
I can thrive

ACKNOWLEDGMENTS

This book would not be the same without the priceless input of two former CIA operatives, who had shown me ways to tell a plausible story without disclosing sensitive information.

Likewise, the story would have lacked color, had it not been for the State Department employee who had been worked at the right embassy in the 1991, and who was able to tell me how that embassy handled cases such as this one.

Thank you for delving back into a pre-digital time, when faxes were still a novelty and U.S. embassy personnel still relied on telegrams, a knowledge of their environment, and gut instinct.

CHAPTER 1

IT ALL HAPPENED so fast. Yesterday, Gina had bought a return train ticket from Skopje, Macedonia. A clean bed in her student apartment in Dubrovnik had been her only goal back then, but life got a lot more complicated within the last hour. Now she was stuck on a crowded train that smelled of old sweat, fermented fish, and coal smoke.

Podgorica, Montenegro. The train had ground to a stop and it didn't look like travel was going to resume anytime soon.

She scanned the faces of her fellow travelers. An old, wrinkled woman dressed in black was traveling with her little grandson, who seemed comfortable enough lounging in the cargo net over her head. They were packed in like cattle by American standards, with people stuck outside in the narrow hallway, sitting on their suitcases.

She envied them. At least they had more elbow room than she did inside her crowded compartment with five adults jammed on the each of the facing hard wooden benches. The space between their knees was taken up by rucksacks and baskets and the two stray suitcases that hadn't fit overhead, across from the kid.

Her butt hurt, she was thirsty, and she still tasted the salty tang of pickled fish that the old woman next to her had shared all around. It hadn't been bad, just pervasive. Like the poverty that surrounded her here - something she noticed every single day.

People around her talked in agitated polyglot of the land. Thirty-two languages were spoken in Yugoslavia, a country that exploded under her sneakered feet like a powder keg.

4

Nobody around her spoke English. In the fall of 1991, in a rural area of the Balkans, English wasn't fashionable. She had managed with her Italian on the Adriatic Coast, but none of her fellow passengers spoke the language and the closest she could get was an older man, whose related Istrian was too guttural to understand. The others found areas of linguistic overlap amongst themselves, leaving her high and dry.

She could tell the common Serbo-Croatian and Slovenian apart most of the time, and she could extrapolate the meaning of some of the words from Russian as long as they were written down, but comprehension of everyday speech still eluded her.

Gina strained her ears for something, anything she might be able to understand. A smattering of Greek, a bit of Albanian, one of the Turk languages from the family two compartments and five hours back, but they may as well have conversed in the twelve languages now extinct on the Balkan peninsula for all the good it did her.

She fretted as the train remained still.

The plan had been to examine several Byzantine frescoes that had survived the earthquakes in a number of churches in Skopje. Armed with her observations and photographs and ready to tackle her thesis, Gina was now thwarted by an antiquated transportation system that was dictated not only by Belgrade as the hub of the dilapidating Yugoslav republic, but also by the sharp, steep mountains that directed traffic through river valleys. Thus, Gina was going to take a train from Skopje to Belgrade, and take her first connection from Belgrade to Podgorica, Montenegro. That would put her back on the Adriatic Coast. She then planned to take the bus up the coast to Dubrovnik, a picturesque city of medieval battlements that occupied a thin sliver of Croatia between Serbia and the sea. The Croatian territory was so narrow, one could cross it on a bicycle in a single, leisurely afternoon.

She wished he had that option despite the encroaching cold. Gina had always gotten in scrapes in chase of high-adrenaline adventures. Having to climb the moutnain pass on a bike would have resulted in zooming down to the sea level on the other side.

The idea thrilled her, granting a temporary respite from her current predicament.

THE PEOPLE AROUND her settled down into an expectant silence. Gina looked out the smudged window, as eager for news as everyone else. A man in a dark uniform approached the train wagon's door and swung up onto the step. The passengers opened a barrage of questions, but fell silent when he gestured for them to calm down. He said a few words in Serbian, but all Gina understood the word 'Dubrovnik'. She watched the people around her stiffen. The old woman sitting across from her closed her eyes, as though resigned to their fate. Most passengers began to talk, their sentences cutting the air with their agitated tones.

"Do you speak English?" Gina asked the man in uniform. He shook his head, and took a wide step over two suitcases on the floor, pushing his way into the compartment. He wavered precariously, leaned his hand against the luggage rack over her head, and looked down at her.

"Passport," he said. His expression was concerned.

She produced her dark blue American passport. He examined it and returned it to her. Then he said something in Serbian, speaking very slowly.

Gina shook her head. "No comprende," she said, hoping the Italian she learned at her grandmother's knee in New Jersey would help.

"Non si può andare a Dubrovnik," he said.

"Perché?" She asked, trying to find out why going back to Dubrovnik was impossible.

"C'è la guerra."

La Guerra. Gina thought hard. The word was familiar, if seldom used in her family. She recalled the kitchen, the relatives, the talk of the old country and the partisans in the mountains above Po valley… of course.

La Guerra meant 'war'.

IT SEEMED PRUDENT to blend in with the natives. The land where Gina was studying old church triptychs and elaborate frescoes painted directly onto vaulted cathedral ceilings turned wild and unpredictable. Group decisions take time even when the participants share a language or several, however, and it took two hours before the travelers decided to empty the train and seek alternate means of transportation.

Stay with the crowd.

At least until she formulated a plan, Gina relied on the second-hand experience of her college professor, Dr. Rita Rofe, who had been doing her graduate work in archeology in El Salvador in the late seventies.

"Stay with the crowd and do your best to look native," Dr. Rofe had said back then, preparing her graduate students for the realities of the changing geopolitical climate. "November 1979 seemed normal enough. You wouldn't have recognized the country by Christmas."

Thus, Gina hoisted the backpack that contained her books, notebooks, and camera onto her back, and she slung the old gym bag over her shoulder. She wore the American student uniform of jeans, sneakers, and a windbreaker and there was no doubt in her mind that there was no way she could fade into the crowd like a local village girl.

This difference had been, so far, a positive one.

Now it might be a liability.

There was no telling if the warring parties viewed Americans in a positive or a negative light. As she walked with the rest of the train passengers down the cracked asphalt of the two-lane road leading toward Podgorica, she focused on analyzing her limited data.

A war broke out.

She knew it would, eventually, which was why she'd been scouring old churches with her camera, cataloguing ancient art in case it was looted or, even worse, destroyed. The warring factions targeted Dubrovnik, a medieval port city where she had her studio apartment. She had to decide where to go, and fast. As she walked, she surveyed the buildings that grew denser around her.

This was the suburbs of Podgorica, then, and the train tracks that ran through it stood jammed with stationary trains. Crowds of pedestrians with their luggage converged from thin streams into a slow river that was like a force unto itself.

She wove her way out of the crowd comfortably, and observed. Her imagination couldn't fit all these people into the small and antiquated Podgorica train station. The rail station boasted all of three passenger rails. The station building loomed old and desolate over the boarding platform.

7

Its interior hid the ubiquitous tobacco stand, and there was a place to buy a snack when they were open, which wasn't very often. Gina would be all too happy to avoid a place whose outdated, concrete-based architecture reminded her of Auschwitz.

This war could never be that bad.

The stray thought startled her. Of course it could. Every war could be as bad and the Balkans were the perfect powder-keg.

Ethnic tensions. Old grievances. Historical feuds.

A dictatorship had suppressed them for several decades, but Tito was dead now. Power abhorred vacuum, and many wanted that power now.

Gina looked at her map. If she took a right turn onto the 13. Jula street toward the Moraca river, it would bring her right under the Gorica hillock and near the church of St. George. The church was in the park, away from the crowds and off the beaten path. She could spend the chilly night inside – couldn't she? It wasn't that cold yet. She could only hope that the church would be open and she could take refuge. Her decision centered on the theory that an army would try to leave churches and other objects of historical and cultural interest intact.

Along the way, Gina met an Italian family whose vacation had taken a turn for the worse. The stranded Italians told her that Dubrovnik was under siege by some hopped-up and ill-understood Serbian expansionist army.

If the Serbs were on the move, she'd best avoid getting in their way. As her legs ate up the pavement between her and her goal, she considered her long-term options.

She could go south – but Albania was hardly a cradle of safety and human rights.

She could go back to Macedonia and cross into Greece. Possible – but not without first going north-east to Belgrade. The as-the-crow-flies direction put the mountains in her way. A train ticket to Greece and a boat fare to Italy would tap her out financially. Never mind her student apartment – Gina travelled light. Her true base of operations was at the Academia di Belle Arti in Ravenna, Italy. They had a cooperative extension program with Cleveland Institute of Art. She used to snicker at being a "CIA agent in Italy," but the resources that would now entail didn't sound all that bad. The acronym for the Cleveland Institute of Art was an old joke

8

with all her friends. The school's cooperative extension program in Europe was a little-known treasure, and she was in one of its outreach programs – and, by extension, in a war zone.

HAD SHE HAD the ready cash, she would have made her way to the Adriatic and bribed a fisherman to take her across to Italy. Eastern Bloc refugees used to do that all the time.

She considered her funds. She had some Yugoslav dinar, which were just about worthless as soon as the first shot had been fired in Dubrovnik.

She did have her two hundred dollar emergency fund, a meager remnant of her former one-thousand dollar reserve. She would have never guessed how quickly the money disappeared in local "gestures of appreciation," which made her life so much easier when trying to gain access to a controlled and highly protected works of art. It was as though the bribery was expected, even required. Thus, going by sea was out of her financial reach.

Going north was, even for her devil-may-care adventuresome spirit, way too dangerous. Serbian forces would cover the area between Serbia and the Adriatic, and Gina didn't like her odds on being able to avoid them. Avoiding troops of any kinds seemed prudent, especially for a young woman. In a foreign country. Alone.

A shiver passed over her shoulders. A wind, perhaps, or a current of cold autumn air that drifted in off the seaa. She attributed her goosebumps to the changeable weather.

Fear was best suppressed.

Panic kills.

Gina took a deep breath, like she'd been taught in dance class in her high school years. Life was just another performance, and all she had do was get through it without disaster, without falling, without throwing up.

She moved her feet, step after step landing on the weathered asphalt road, muffled by her well-worn shoes. She breathed in, and out, nice and deep.

Breathe the panic out.

9

It worked, just like it had worked before her performances, or exams, or rock-climbing adventures. The lighter and more centered feeling soothed her pounding heart, and let the air ease in and out of her lungs. Evening mist began to fall, and her mouth puckered at the astringent, clean tannin smell of leaf decay that surrounded the tall chestnut trees.

The simple stone walls of the square church tower rose before her in the dusk of the coming night. She cut through the park and under the trees, lifting her feet to keep from making noise in the fallen leaves. She hoped the old church would still be open.

CHAPTER 2

Peter glanced at Vera. She was frowning, watching the small town pass by through the bullet-proof window of their black Mercedes.

Podgorica was beautiful in the morning twilight. The sun had not yet crested the mountains to the East, and the yellow leaves were giving way to rust. The illusion of aquarelle peace was but a lie despite the bright terra cotta roofs gleaming on white stucco buildings. Residential neighborhoods queued their way up the hills, and the Moraca River carved a navigable valley between them on its way to the Adriatic. If it weren't for the traffic jam of trains that could go no further, and for the throngs of stranded travelers sleeping in the streets around the rail station, Podgorica would have presented the very image of peaceful dawn.

"I can't believe they're shooting up Dubrovnik." Vera's anger and frustration poured out in a wave.

Words swept over him like the surf breaking on the beach, hardly making a visible impact. He took note of his wife's anger, shifted around a few sand grains, but remained otherwise unaffected.

Peter had acknowledged, long ago, that Vera had boundless passion for her work. As much as he supported her in her efforts to save ancient artifacts from the ravages of an encroaching war zone, he found that it was best not to get swept up in the wake of her zeal.

He remained calm. He was, after all, a mere catalyst who made things happen. Getting overwrought by his wife's artistic and humanitarian passions did not advance his Uncle Ilya's goals. That's not to say that Peter's goals were perfectly aligned with those of his criminally inclined family. His personal goal was to make Vera happy.

The family seemed to think that Peter was the fulcrum through which to increase weapons sales in yet another unstable geopolitical area. In his own eyes, he wanted to be the catalyst that propelled his amazing wife to a position of academic prestige she so richly deserved. If that meant touring a war zone in search of stolen and endangered art, he was happy to extend his considerable resources and make it so.

Their driver turned into the park and navigated under the almost-bare trees. The old church and its tall, rectangular bell tower appeared as though out of nowhere.

At least this place was well hidden.

Peter checked his .45 caliber Glock and glanced to the side.

Vera slid a round into the chamber of her 9 mm Beretta.

Their bodyguard got out of the front passenger seat, holding his own handgun down by his leg. First he surveyed the area, then he nodded at the two identical cars behind them.

A driver and a passenger disembarked from each.

Their suits and ties, together with the black, official-looking vehicles, gave their caravan a diplomatic feel, making their passage through checkpoints possible without having to lubricate their way with wasteful amounts of bribe money.

Peter's men established a perimeter around the St. George's church, falling into a well-worn pattern. It was an old, Byzantine-style basilica and it contained art that was both priceless and open to theft.

He'd secure the area.

She'd rescue art from a war zone, catalogue it, analyze it and keep it safe until all this blew over. Doing so would further boost her significant professional status.

The biggest problem, as far as Peter was concerned, was that the public thought this little spat would blow over fast. This was the Balkans. Its multiple ethnicities had been spoiling for a fight ever since the Ottoman Empire fell apart. The Hapsburgs had to rule it with an iron hand. World War I had been launched from Sarajevo with the assassination of the Hapsburg crown prince Ferdinand de Este. World War II had turned the craggy, arid hills of the Balkans into a hotbed of partisan activity that had never allowed the Germans let their guards down, and President Tito had come out of this crucible as both Yugoslavia's savior and iron-fisted dictator. From the end of the war until his death in 1980, Tito had bludgeoned the minorities into getting along by force of personality as well as force of arms.

A faraway clang of train cars, a screech of steel against steel, reminded Peter they better hustle. There were people out there, people who might drift in this direction

The same sort of people the world had expected to rise at Tito's death. The world had waited for the inevitable explosion of old hurts with bated breath, but the fuse had been surprisingly long. The Sarajevo Winter Olympics in 1984 were a love-fest of the first order and an ostentatious display of brotherhood. Everyone seemed to be getting along so well – perhaps too well for it to be true. Few years later, Slovenia declared independence, then Croatia, and now Serbia decided to reclaim their access to the Adriatic by capturing the port of Dubrovnik.

Those same people were out there, bearing arms, laying claims to old hurts that had festered like wounds for decades. Centuries.

Peter pressed his lips together and exchanged a hand signal with one of his guards.

They were ready. At his wife's questioning look, he forced an exhale.

"All clear. Let's get this show on the road."

THE CHURCH was supposed to be locked up, but the old, wooden door opened at Vera's first pull. She gave a careful exhale.

"What?"

"It's unlocked. We're too late."

"Maybe, maybe not," Peter whispered and gestured to his men as he pulled Vera against the rough stone wall. She stayed plastered right where he put her for now, feeling the cold stone drain her body heat.

The men entered with guns drawn. It strucked her funny, all of a sudden, that they would enter a church the same way they always entered their hotel room.

Securing it.

If there was one aspect of life with her new husband, this constant need for bodyguards was something she could do without. Vera liked shooting enough – it was a lot of fun, making holes in a paper target, always improving her score. She didn't like to carry, though. Her gun never seemed concealed enough on her curves despite her lanky body. Rather than feeling secure, she always feared she would buckled under the weight of responsibility on her shoulders.

Don't leave the gun in the bathroom.
Don't show the gun in the restaurant.
Don't wear a skimpy dress where the gun would show.

The most important imperative was not losing control of her weapon and have it turned against her.

As much as Vera disliked this necessary aspect of Peter's work, she was grateful that his travel schedule and resources allowed her to go on art rescue forays. She relished beating whole gangs of international smugglers to the punch. Nobody knew – not yet – but her efforts would be well rewarded years from now, when all the art was returned.

When the war was over.

She, too, felt the weight of history behind what seemed, at first, to be just a petty ethnic skirmish. They talked of little else.

She thought they'd be cleared for entry any moment. Then she heard a woman scream from within the church.

VERA LAUNCHED herself into the maw of the open church door, only to feel Peter grab her arm and yank her back.

"Stay here." He didn't bother to hide his irritation.

"That didn't sound like an art thief," she snapped back.

"Don't be naïve. Just because she's female doesn't make her harmless."

"Funny, hearing that from you," Vera mused as she relaxed into his grip and leaned against his chest. Peter's opinion of women kept evolving with every encounter. When they had met, Peter had been a playboy. He had a girl or two in every major city and made no secret of the fact that he wasn't ready to settle down. Falling in love with Vera came as a surprise to him back then, and not necessarily a welcome one.

Vera had faced a choice back then - accept Peter in an open relationship, or scare him away. She had thought he was way out of her league as it was. Vera had thought of herself as mousy, boring, and unattractive – the very opposite of her cheerleader sister.

Peter was still a playboy and his worldliness made him interesting. He had a way of listening to whatever Vera had to say with all of his being, just as he had a way of dropping suggestions that offered Vera new avenues and opportunities. Then he would sit back and watch the fruit of his labors blush with its pregnant potential.

Vera in a designer night gown. Vera in graduate school. Vera abroad, speaking foreign languages.

He declared his firm opinion that she could do anything in the world, and did so repeatedly. He opened doors and offered connections to make it so. He was the sunshine to her growth. She loved him for it, and she loved him for staying with her even though he surrounded himself with actresses and models who made Vera look like she worked for the hotel's room service.

Anonymous, forgettable, average.

Vera used to think that Peter's profligate screwing around was nothing but a sign of disrespect for both himself and for women in general. Over time, her understanding had developed into a stoic acceptance of the fact that the man who professed to love her simply suffered the worst case of zipper malfunction imaginable. Women, the obviously gorgeous ones, were his Persian flaw, his Achilles' heel.

Now, when she heard her husband refer to women as dangerous art thieves, Vera was buoyed by the small victory. It seemed that she had done much to change his mind about the nature of the "weaker sex."

"ALL CLEAR." Louis stuck his head out the church door and waved them in. As Peter and Vera entered, she noticed Peter still pressed his hand against the holster of his gun. Vera took a step in and then a few steps to the side of the ancient structure. Now that she stopped being a big fat target in the lit doorway, she stopped to let her eyes adjust.

15

Light filtered in through the narrow windows, leaving the wall decorations in relative darkness. She saw the old frames and the cross above the altar. A triptych, consisting of three painted panels, stood against the back wall with a tall candlestick on each side. The metal under the pale wax looked black in the dim light, and Vera wondered whether they were old, silver ones that became tarnished due to air pollution, or whether the silver had already been stolen and the church replaced them with cast-iron look-alikes.

She took note of the objects within the church with a swift, sweeping glance before she let her eyes rest on the thief.

Two of Peter's men held a young woman by her upper arms while the third one emptied the contents of her bags and set them on the dark pew. A camera, rolls upon rolls of film, notebooks...

Vera looked the woman up and down. She was a bit shorter than herself and her hair had blonde highlights, as though from the sun. She wore jeans and sneakers. Possibly an American, then. Nobody in Europe wore tennis shoes unless they intended to play tennis.

"What's your name?" Vera asked in a neutral tone of voice.

"None of your business," the woman said as she struggled against the men who still held her.

Vera picked up a notebook.

"Hey, put that down. That's mine." There was no mistaking the anger in the captive's voice.

"I'm just looking," Vera said calmly, and opened the notebook to a random page. She found a technical drawing of an old, broken wall. There was an inner wall and an outer wall, and the space in-between was filled with loose gravel. The construction method was typical of a region not far from here. The drawing was annotated in tight, careful handwriting, and the language was English.

"I see you got to visit Macedonia," Vera commented as she turned the page. The notes that filled it were interspersed with an alpha-numeric code. "FF-19." Vera's voice hummed over the coded information. "FF-20. Oh, I see. You are referring to the photograph on a particular roll of film? Very good."

"My name is Gina Francesca Migliore, and you could tell your dumb goons to let me go. This church doesn't have anything for you to steal anyway. I talked to the priest already."

Vera looked up from the notebook. "Gina, is it? I am Vera." She returned to the notebook, leafed through it, and then she set it down and picked up another one. The subject matter was slightly different, but the note-taking style indicated the same author. "Are you a student, then?" Vera asked.

"Sort of." Gina seemed somewhat recalcitrant."

"Okay." Vera looked at Peter. He wore a disinterested gaze, but she knew nothing escaped him. "Tell them to let her go, Peter. She's a student."

"How'd you know? Her notes?"

"Yeah, either art history or architecture." Vera watched in satisfaction as Peter nodded at his men. They let go of Gina immediately. She shook herself off and rubbed her arms. Then she glared at her captors and her companions, as though to commit their faces to memory.

"You could tell just from my notebook?" She asked Vera.

Vera gave an apologetic shrug. "I'm sorry. We thought you were here to take things."

"You mean, you figured I'm a… a church robber? What the hell? Are Americans really known for stealing antiquities from old churches in these parts?" Gina sputtered and gesticulated. Vera was amused to see the younger woman drew herself to make most of her shorter stature.

"I study art history, and I teach English to supplement my grad school scholarship! If you or your dumb gorillas here knew a single thing about the cultural significance and the artistic value of these paintings," Vera watched Gina wave around the space expansively, "or about that unassuming little diptych over there, you'd realize I have no motivation to steal any of this stuff."

Vera leaned her butt against a wooden pew and waited until Gina ran out of steam. She glanced at Peter, who returned her look with an expression of utter glee. She knew Peter lived for situations such as these. He loved to instigate, outsmart, and one-up in every single area of his life. When he couldn't do so, he just blended into the background and observed, collecting information. Once he had enough data and context, he

17

proceeded to instigate until he created an opening for a perfect one-up scene. No matter what the environment, he always managed to carry it off looking like a perfect gentleman.

The church fell silent for a whole minute while Vera let the younger woman simmer. She was pretty, with brown hair that still bore the remnants of the summer sun's highlights, and seemed athletic in the way most women in their twenties are. Her clothing was "generic American," but not tourist. Gina was dressed as a practical traveler, probably no stranger to sleeping in odd places, and she travelled light. Vera diverted her attention from her and walked over to the side altar.

The wood of its main structure was pitted by woodworm and darkened with age. The diptych that sat upon its table surface consisted of two rectangular frames carved of old wood, joined by a brass hinge. The frames displayed paintings of saints.

Vera assessed the artifact with an experienced eye. She had studied many an icon for her thesis, but she specialized in Kievan work, not in things that came from this end of the former Ottoman Empire. She turned toward Gina and flashed a wry smile. "Forgive my ignorance here, but what exactly is so special about these two little paintings?"

GINA TURNED toward the woman that came with the goons. Now that she got to see her from behind, she was all too aware of the small pistol in the waistband of her trousers. She was taller, looked stronger, and had more resources than Gina had at the moment. Her English sounded American enough, but that was no guarantee of good intentions.

"It's of no great financial value," she said with a shrug. "It's local, though. The figure on the right represents Saint Basil of Ostrog. See? If you could read Cyrillic, you'd be able to see it on the upper left of his head."

Gina was surprised to see the woman pull out a small flashlight and inspect the gilded background and its red-ink inscription.

"You can generally tell him by his book, the vestments of a bishop, and the hat and beard, Gina continued. "He was born in Herzegovina in the – oh – seventeenth century."

"He was born on December 12th, 1610, actually," the taller woman said. "And the figures on the left panel?"

"That's just a standard Madonna and Child representation. It's stylistically different from what I'd expect, though, and that makes it interesting."

The older woman straightened her back and turned to face Gina. "How so?"

Gina shrugged again. She hated the nervous gesture. It wasn't the questioning she minded, or the strangers, or even their guns. She hated that an unfamiliar situation would erode her usual confidence with such casual ease. Gina drew herself up, and leaned forward in a struggle to regain her footing. "It's just a few little things… the rendition of the faces and their proportion reminds me of early Italian Renaissance. It doesn't have that typical "Jesus as a miniature adult" look. He's more cherubic and their faces are more emotive. Look at the eyes!" Her excitement began to rise as she neared the diptych and her unusual examiner, every step inbued with slightly more ease.

"What do you see?" The question drifted in a soft, quiet voice that barely stirred the still air within the ancient structure.

"I think the piece was commissioned from Italy. It's a travel altar, but it's Orthodox, and Italy was Catholic."

"Or, it's by someone who studied in Italy," Vera said. "The world came to Italy to learn about many a thing. Especially art." There was something reverent in the older woman's voice.

"Who are you, anyway?" Gina asked.

"I am Dr. Avery Christoff. Most people call me Vera."

Gina jumped back and looked her up and down. Her brown hair was tied back and she was taller than Gina would have expected her to be. She looked different in her sensible travel clothes – very different from the pictures in the society pages of Italian rags, or in the special occasion photos that populated professional literature. "You are *the* Dr. Christoff? The one who wrote that paper on the Kievan icons? The one that was working with the Louvre on the return of those stolen pieces…" Gina saw an ironic quirk of Vera's lips, and stopped the torrent of her words.

"Yes. I am."

CHAPTER 3

Gina took a step back as though somebody pushed her in the chest. "You are Dr. Christoff." She sounded incredulous and a bit stupid, repeating herself. "You know, the *intellectual* Dr. Avery Christoff?"

A sharp bark of laughter split the air behind her. Gina spun, facing the man in charge. He was as tall as his wife, which made him average, since Dr. Christoff was a tall woman. He seemed to be in his mid-thirties and wore brown slacks and a tan zip-up jacket. It gaped open right now, showing the straps of a shoulder holster peeking from under the edge. Gina speculated that that's where he must have put the gun that he had been carrying as they both came in.

He grinned at her. "Sorry for the rough greeting. So…" he looked her up and down. She just knew her cheeks colored with heat. "You're an American student and I figure you got stranded, right?"

"That's right." Gina didn't feel inclined to let him know more than absolutely necessary. There was something about him, something unusual and exotic that hinted at danger and Hollywood action movies. Something… enticing.

"Look, we'll talk to the priest here and make sure the artwork's properly secured, and then we'll be off. Do you need a ride? Where did you want to go?"

Gina walked over to her open backpack and her duffel bag without a reply. She started to put her things back, making sure nothing was missing.

"Look… what's your name again?" Dr. Avery Christoff spoke up almost behind her.

"Gina," she said, not looking away from her task.

21

"I understand why you'd feel uncomfortable in our company," Dr. Christoff continued, "but I'd suggest you weigh your options. We can easily give you a ride out of what's about to become a war zone. If you choose to decline, we can direct you to the local police department, who will probably put you in a refugee camp. They will do their best to notify the US embassy… when they get around to it. At this stage you could be stuck here for quite a long time."

Gina zipped up her bags, straightened up, and turned.

"How do I know you're the real Dr. Christoff?"

Vera didn't smile. "Good point. Here." She fished inside her blazer and unzipped a security pocket. "Here's my passport."

She handed it over. Gina took it and opened the dark blue booklet. It looked just like hers, and the plastic laminate that covered the photograph and the identifying information appeared genuine. The woman in the picture looked a bit younger, too. That reassured Gina. The passport wasn't made in someone's basement yesterday.

Gina handed it back. "Okay. Thank you. But I do have to ask – why do you travel with armed guards?"

One of the silent men stirred at that, but Dr. Christoff only laughed. "Celebrity status. It's just a routine precaution, but since I have the best protection money can buy, I try to do some good with it. There's been a rash of church robberies throughout the former Eastern Bloc. Those countries lost an amazing number of artifacts. Silver candlestick holders, censors, paintings, crosses – even fairly large statues from gardens, castles. Even graveyards."

"Who steals it?" Gina asked. She did hear rumors of art theft and smuggling, but it had been connected to the Middle East.

"The locals, usually," Dr. Christoff shrugged. "They've been poor for so long, it's a chance to make a buck. It used to be state property, all of it. They'd come up with an interesting saying: 'If you don't steal from the state, you steal from your own family'." She paused, letting the words sink. "And since all art over there belonged to the state, once the dictatorial regime fell, many a lowlife saw an opportunity. They were free to travel abroad now and sold the goods to wealthy Westerners. It was very entrepreneurial of them."

"You seem to be very matter-of-fact about it," Gina remarked.

22

"There's not much I can do about human nature, but I can always take precautions. So. Will you join us?"

"Where're you going next?" Gina asked.

"We are headed to Vienna. You could hop on a train to Italy as soon as we clear the border, or you can come all the way, if you want. Whatever you feel is safest at the time." Dr. Christoff smiled, and her grey eyes crinkled in warm welcome. "This could be an adventure of a lifetime, you know."

Gina nodded seriously, but her heart stirred with the promise of excitement. She looked toward the woman's husband. He nodded acquiescence. She avoided looking at the guards, though, because she didn't need *their* permission. "Thank you, then. It will be a pleasure to join you."

THEY STOPPED at six more churches on the way north. Neither visit took more than half an hour. Two ancient structures were already devoid of valuables, and Gina saw Vera give the priest in charge some kind of printed information.

Vera and Peter.

She rolled the names in her mind as she waited for them outside an old chapel. Gina already had a look at the interior – a standard Romanesque design – and as there were no antiquities to protect, she left Vera to her conversation. It was nice to get out of the car for a little while. She hid from the persistent drizzle by pressing her back against the wall, where she was mostly protected by the eaves. The sandy texture of the whitewashed stucco dug through the fabric of on her shoulders and as she inhaled, she detected a hint of old frankincense. The wooden door to her right was dark with age and numerous layers of stain, but the metal of its hardware gleamed with newness.

Vera and Peter.

They were an unusual couple, and she was flattered when they invited her to be on a first-name basis. It turned out that she and Vera shared common roots in New Jersey, although neither lived there anymore. They traded stories of their vastly different neighborhoods. Vera grew up in the academic Princeton, whereas Gina was all Jersey City, with an Italian grandmother who formed a part of the traditional melting pot package.

Gina was pleased to find her Italian was a lot better than Vera's, but when she heard Peter and Vera speak in casual and fluent Russian, something stopped her from confessing that she understood most of what they said. It wasn't a sense of caution as much as shyness. Gina considered Russian to be one of her worst languages. Her grasp of grammar was so full of holes, she felt self-conscious whenever she had to open her mouth and put a Russian sentence together. She always wondered whether she used the proper gender for each noun and whether she declenated her adjectives just so – and the fact that the bitchy exchange student from St. Petersburg had laughed her head off at her efforts didn't help one bit.

The memory rankled, especially since the girl's English had been nearly flawless back then, with just a hint of an accent that the young men around her found exotic. Gina shut her mouth and stretched her ears in an effort to hear what real, unrehearsed Russian sounded like. Maybe she would learn and improve from this brief exposure.

"I am sorry, we should speak English with you around. It's hardly fair otherwise," Peter had said at breakfast. "We speak Russian at home a lot, and Vera did her thesis research in Kiev. She likes to keep in practice."

"Your Italian is fluent, so maybe you should travel more," Peter had suggested over lunch later that day. He had been courteous, pulling out her chair and ordering the best local dishes for her to try. He was charming, undeniably attractive, and had a way of listening with his whole being, as though whatever Gina said, or what she was interested in at the time, fascinated him completely. She felt like she was drawn into the pools of his warm, brown eyes. His smile put her completely at ease.

It felt dangerous. She knew she was getting a bit too close to feeling flattered by a married man. Worse, his wife was the prominent and influential Dr. Christoff, who could absolutely ruin Gina's career if she took exception at any sign of flirtation between the two of them.

Besides, Dr. Christoff was now Vera to her, and Gina liked Vera a lot. She liked her wry humor and her realistic assessment of situations where her husband was nothing but cheerful optimism. Hurting Vera was definitely something Gina strove to avoid. She glanced at her every so often, trying to gauge her reaction to Peter's attentive behavior. Yet as the three of them sat around the table and Peter once again plied Gina with his attentive gestures, Vera just leaned back in her chair and observed their interaction with a bemused smile.

THE COUNTRYSIDE LOOKED arid and rugged, beautiful in its stark, Mediterranean way. Their caravan wended down the narrow, foggy mountain passes when it began to rain later that afternoon. Gina tried to recall what she knew of ancient history of the area.

She could easily imagine half-naked warriors with bronze swords and shields march through the mists of time on roads they had built two thousand years ago. There'd be supply wagons and tents, and metal smiths to repair armor. To sharpen the swords necessary to conquer this or that far-flung kingdom, a place that was now a country with fewer than three main languages and a political system that struggled to approach what the West would call "fairness."

The descendants of these warriors walked these roads now. Some were minding ordinary business. Others wore army fatigues and carried machine guns. Vera and Peter led their small caravan in a half-circle east of Dubrovnik, well out of the way of the Serbian siege. Even so, Gina heard the deep rumbling of exploding shells carry on the wind.

She shuddered to think what would become of the medieval port city. She was still on the fence on whether Dubrovnik was stark or quaint in its beauty and now she feared she'd never get to make up her mind. Its white houses and terracotta roofs lent structure to the steep mountainsides above the harbor, forming convoluted streets that perched above the waves of the Adriatic. The medieval castle, the churches, the old city walls – all that was but a fragile target to modern armaments.

The guns were pointed away from her, for which she was grateful. The action seemed focused on Dubrovnik - for now. Occasional roadblock check-points indicated a state of unrest – if not a full-out war – but Gina couldn't tell whose army occupied the territory. The flow of family-packed cars with bundles tied to their rooftops indicated that people were leaving the area to the West, rather than gravitating towards it. The soldiers at the checkpoints let them through at first, but as they moved further north, passage through checkpoints became a lengthy negotiation process. Twice, Peter was forced to step out of the car and have a word with the guards. He had to reach into his side pocket and Gina saw money change hands before they were let through.

THEY WERE in Serbia now. Without realizing she was doing it, Gina shrank into herself in the back seat in an effort to become invisible as they approached their next checkpoint. Artifacts salvaged from two unattended churches weighed heavily in the trunks of the other two cars now, hidden in old boxes and nestled in straw. She was curious to see if their cars would be searched, and if so, if the items they carried would cause any issues.

Yet, to her surprise, Peter showed none of the former sense of apprehension as they approached the Serbian checkpoint. Vera seemed merely resigned. They pulled up and Peter's driver rolled down his window. Peter handed the driver a letter, the driver passed it on to the guard, the guard checked it over and returned it, and let them through. Just like that. It took less than two minutes and it didn't cost a single dinar.

Questions began to roil in Gina's mind. How come the Serbs let them through? They had stopped everyone else. That much was for certain. Yet, in their case, the letter Peter produced had saved them a lengthy delay, and there had been no need to bribe anyone.

She was lit with curiosity. What did the letter say? She wanted to see it, to know what it was. Peter didn't speak Serbian with the men – she was pretty sure she heard a word or two of Russian – but Gina hadn't heard enough to pick up the general gist of the conversation.

Gina was fairly certain that the Christoffs had been using Russian to maintain a veil of privacy in her company. Aside from being tempted to eavesdrop on them for curiosity's sake, she decided that her unusual circumstances allowed for the kinds of practicalities she wouldn't allow herself to indulge in what she viewed as her "regular life." She didn't know these people, and despite Dr. Christoff's credentials, she was not at all sure what would happen to the artifacts they carried from the war zone.

26

They were strangers, and she was stranded. Information was power that would help her control the way her circumstances developed and Gina stretched her ears to pick up every word.

She had done her best to assist Vera's effort at cataloguing and packaging the artifacts they salvaged from unsecured locations. Her professional curiosity drove her to memorize the identifying feature of every item. The small, framed paintings, crosses, and statuettes were certainly quite valuable in both historical and monetary terms.

Something didn't add up, though. Despite the commendable mission of saving artwork from being destroyed inside a developing war zone, there was no explanation for being let through the Serbian checkpoint on just a letter alone. Gina wasn't so naïve to think that the Serbian government would put a high value on antiquities from Montenegro and Croatia. Their passage was eased on account of something else.

THEY STOPPED in the small town of Zabljak that apparently saw a good bit of tourist trade. It sat in a valley on a river so small it would've been a creek, had its flow not been swollen with the recent rains. Angry, roiling waters churned as they fought their way down the too-narrow bed, skipping over boulders. Branches and man-made artifacts were carried on the current, forming jammed dams in the narrow passage between the boulders, holding the waters back – at least until they broke. The banks were held by scrub, grass, and the occasional sapling, and a cast-iron railing divided the sidewalk from the unkempt greenery.

Peter said something to his driver, and Gina strained to make sense of the words. The driver apparently disagreed, and the flow of Russian gained in both volume and speed, well past the point of Gina's comprehension. She turned her eyes to Vera, who gave her a reassuring smile.

"They are arguing over hotels."

"Why?" Gina asked.

"Our bodyguards are particular when it comes to security. They want a defensible location, not a luxurious one. Don't worry, this is normal."

As Vera turned away to follow the argument, and to add to it, Gina began to wonder why was it normal to seek a defensible location to begin with. She began to pick out more words, such as *hotel, pension,* and *idiot,* and realized that the issue was not only a defensible location, but also one large enough to contain a party of eight.

Once the argument died down, their driver led the other two cars away from the town center. The medieval city was situated around a central square area with an impressive statue in the middle, which Gina recognized as yet another black plague monument. The modern– if cracked with neglect – asphalt pavement of the road that connected the towns they had passed through had long given way to the bumpy, quaint, historical discomfort of ancient cobblestones.

In the dim light of the encroaching evening, Gina recognized an outline of a large building with a clock. Probably a city hall. The opposing end of the square was anchored by a church whose cupola was topped with a Greek Orthodox cross. The building that surrounded the square had lovely, ornamental façades with apartments on the upper two or three floors, and with storefronts on the street level. The stores were closed with the exception of what seemed to have been one or two restaurants.

"This looks quite pretty," Gina said in Vera's direction. "Will we have any time to look around tomorrow?"

"Sure. There isn't much to secure in this area, anyway," Vera said. Gina noticed her stormy expression. "This area probably won't become part of the war zone."

"How do you know that?" Gina asked.

"Because we're well into Serbia now. The opposing forces are unlikely to come this far." Gina heard Vera sigh in the darkness, and was about to add something, when Peter interrupted her.

"Don't worry about these things," he said in his calm, encouraging voice. "You worry about saving the artwork, and I'll worry about everything else."

"Like getting us rooms?" Vera asked in a lighter tone.

"Yes. In fact, here we are."

THEY WERE only two blocks away from the square, but getting there took some doing. The large vehicles didn't fit through the quirky, narrow streets of the historical quarter and had to take a detour and stick to the surrounding main streets. The hotel itself was adjoined to other buildings on both sides, and was three stories tall just like the rest of the block. The front door was sheltered by a blue canopy that said "Adria" in white cursive.

They stepped out of the cars, and both Gina and Vera collected their backpacks and duffle bags. Two bodyguards escorted them and Peter inside while the other three drove off to park the vehicles.

"Won't someone break into the cars?" Gina asked Vera in a low voice. The trunks were loaded with antiques, and the polished make of the cars would certainly draw attention.

"There's a walled courtyard nearby," Very whispered. "The guys will take turns standing guard."

"Not that it's really necessary," Peter chimed in. "But, they offered." And Gina wondered why five armed guards, who were driving an art professor and her rich husband around, felt the need to keep an eye on their cars round the clock. As she walked up the wide marble staircase behind Vera and Peter, she thought back to the letter. Once again she wondered what was in it, and how come they were let through with such expedient courtesy.

CHAPTER 4

Gina looked around her room. Two single beds were pushed together, European style, a small desk with a chair, and a wardrobe made of carved wood. There was a communal bath at the end of the hallway, and the toilet was in a separate little room as was customary in Europe.

As she examined the texture of the cool, whitewashed walls, Gina felt transported hundreds of years into the past. She noticed the two-foot wall thickness as she passed through the doors. The building was ancient, and built to last, just like the rest of the little town.

She made sure the bath was empty before she gathered a clean change of clothing and slipped out. There was no shower, but the claw foot bathtub was generous and hot water was plentiful. Gina didn't spend as much time as she would have wished – just getting clean took precedence over a leisurely soak. Maybe later, in the middle of the night, she could sacrifice an hour of sleep. Nobody would want the bathtub then.

She grinned. The water buoyed her body as well as her spirits. She made good use of the bit of shampoo she had left and inhaled its fresh scent as she reclined in the hot water. Gina reviewed the events of the day and reflected upon her traveling companions.

She liked the Christoffs, she really did. She adored Vera. Had they been at the same university, Gina would have gone out of her way to make sure that Dr. Vera Christoff was her advisor. If she couldn't swing that, then at least her informal mentor. The woman was brilliant and determined, and her experienced eye picked out the minutest detail and linked it to historical influences in a way Gina could only dream about. She was on a sabbatical now, but had an undergraduate teaching position waiting for her at Emory University.

Her husband, Peter, came across as an action hero of some sort. He was good-looking in an enticing, bad-ass kind of way, and his brown eyes warmed Gina whenever he showed interest in anything she had to say. Then there were his courteous gestures, accompanied by small touches on her arms, her shoulders. Had he not been married, she would have taken those as a come-on.

Except Vera had been sitting right there, watching them with a small, knowing smile. Gina sighed and pulled the plug, letting the water out. As the cooler air of the room hit her wet and flushed skin, she faced an unpleasant realization. She was immensely attracted to Vera Christoff's husband.

FIFTEEN MINUTES LATER she was back in her room, dressed in her other pair of trousers – which were cleaner – and a button-down shirt and was putting away her dirty clothes when she heard a knock on the window.

Gina spun. She felt like a startled cat, except not nearly as graceful. She dropped the dirty jeans on the floor and fumbled around for an improvised weapon. Another knock shook the glass pane.

"Gina. It's me."

She recognized the muffled voice of Peter Christoff. She also realized she was in the third story of an ancient building. Alarmed, she rushed to the window and pulled the lacy curtain aside. Peter stood on a balcony with an apologetic smile. The window, it turned out, was not a window but a French door with only the top half filled with glass panes. Gina turned a skeleton key in its lock. As she opened the old, wooden door, she noted its cracked white paint that had helped it blend into the wall.

"Peter?"

"Sorry to startle you," he said with a mischievous smile. "Have you seen the terraces yet? No? Come see, while we still have some light." He beckoned her outside and she followed him. The air was cool and the mountain breeze stripped what warmth there was left from her bath, sending a shiver through her body.

"I didn't know there was a balcony," she said.

"There is, and the individual rooms have their own privacy here. These dividing walls are new since last time I'd been here." He pointed at the solid stucco to either side of them. "The view is quite nice, isn't it?"

Gina shivered again as she took in the colors of the sunset. Darkness was only minutes away. "How did you get up here?"

"I climbed up the trellis," Peter said with an easy shrug. "But you're freezing. Let's get you inside. I just thought you would have wanted to know about this little gem. Whenever we stay here in the summer, we always spend some time on the terrace in the evening."

Gina took two steps toward the waist-high stone wall. Its stucco matched the rest of the building, although its top was capped with tiles. A single look down revealed the top of a wooden structure, most of which was covered with vines. The few leaves that were left were dry and brown in the dimming light of the encroaching evening.

"I didn't know grapes can grow as high up as this," Gina said as she turned to Peter.

"They do. They're also quite delicious." He slipped out of his jacket and draped it over Gina's shoulders. She felt his hand brush her ear, her neck.

"Your hair is wet. No wonder you're cold. Let's turn in. Come on!" She felt Peter's hand in the small of her back as he ushered her back inside her room, and a moderate sense of guilt flooded her as she enjoyed the body heat that seeped through the thin fabric of his nylon jacket. He closed the door, then he turned toward her and rubbed her arms with his hands.

"Sorry about that. I didn't realize you just stepped out of the bath," he said.

"That's okay." The space between them was just a few inches now, and Peter emanated heat and comfort and something else.

She knew she should have excused herself and ushered him out her door. "Why are you here?" she asked instead.

Their eyes met, and Peter bent his head down until his lips landed on Gina's forehead. The kiss could have been friendly, almost chaste, the way European kisses often were.

It wasn't.

"I came here to tell you about my wife and I." His hands were still on Gina's arms, warming them. She felt the connection down to the toes of her feet.

"W... what about Vera?" Her question had many layers. She didn't intend to phrase it quite like that.

"Vera and I have an understanding. We love one another very much, but we both accept my need to appreciate women in their variety and charm." He paused as though to gauge her reaction. Then he leaned his head closer in and continued. "Vera approves of you, you know."

"I could never do this to her." Gina's voice felt hollow, as though someone else had uttered the words.

"Can you do this *for* her, though? For both of us? If it pleases you, of course." Peter Christoff let a practiced smile bloom on his face and pulled Gina into a gentle embrace.

She inhaled. She could smell him now as well as feel his body heat. Notes of musk and cinnamon and something deep and primal made themselves known, and to her alarm she felt her body relax against Peter just enough to return his gesture. She thought back to all those little niceties of his, and of the pleasure she felt in Vera's company as they catalogued old artifacts together.

She vacillated.

She looked up. Their lips met.

Peter's lips were soft and dry. Her nose picked up just a hint of shaving cream. It was late in the day, and Peter took the trouble to shave before he climbed up the trellis to see her. It made her smile. They were well into the best kiss of her life.

But Vera...

What kind of an understanding was Peter talking about?

They should stop. She should stop.

But the warmth, the soft caress – the way she fit against Peter, shorter and smaller.

Peter's phone went off. They broke apart and Gina drew a sharp breath to regain her composure. She let it out in a steady stream, relieved at the interruption as he pulled his phone out of his pocket and checked the number.

"Sorry, I have to get this," he said in his most apologetic voice.

Once again Gina noted how very charming he was. Smooth. Almost professional, if there was such a thing. How many women did he sample with Vera's permission? There was a slick quality to him, something that Gina hadn't noticed before and didn't want to analyze just then. That kiss had been, after all, amazing.

She turned toward the balcony to give Peter some privacy. He spoke Russian. By now, Gina's ear had adjusted enough and she was able to pick up most of the conversation. Peter was meeting someone at one o'clock in the morning, behind the gate, and he had the goods.

VERA HEARD THE door open and close as Peter eased his way into the room. He was as silent as a fog drifting in from the sea. There had been a time when Vera would have pretended to already be asleep.

This time, however, a different game was afoot. Something else, something threatening. Gina wasn't just another piece of grab-ass that her husband required on regular basis. She was too much like herself, except younger. Plain, with shoulder-length brown hair and the student uniform of jeans, sneakers, and practical tops that didn't need to be dry-cleaned or ironed.

Much like herself, Gina was smart and showed significant academic potential. Had she been just a local socialite with an hour-glass figure and cosmetically enhanced body parts, Vera would have pretended to almost-wake as Peter slithered back to bed, and they would have embraced and exchanged their good-night kisses. Next morning, Vera would be the lucky beneficiary of her husband's insatiable libido. Except Gina was different from the other women, and this stark contrast made her stomach churn and her jaw tighten.

She and Peter had a deal. He got to play the field, but only as long as he always came back to the homestead. Perhaps it was time to revisit the terms of their agreement, however, and revise the nature of their relationship.

Instead of pretending to be asleep to save face, like she'd always done, Vera sat in bed, propped up with two pillows. Her miniscule reading light was attached to a clipboard that held a printout of yet another obscure academic paper.

She heard Peter stop in his tracks.

Vera suppressed a smile. Then she removed her reading glasses and looked up at her startled husband.

"I see you're back. Was she any good?"

He shrugged. There was a long pause before he said anything. "We've been married for five years and this is the first time you ask a question like that."

"I see you're not answering my question, but I guess that's okay. You know I like our young Gina. She's a promising young woman." She softened her expression, and as she expected, she saw Peter's shoulders relax.

"She's that. If she's interested in art smuggling in the Middle East, I could hook her up with a guy I know on Cyprus. Do you think she's adventurous enough to actually go there?"

Peter's run of jumbled sentences spoke of unexpected relief. Vera had wanted to talk about his need to fuck other women, but it seemed that this wasn't a time of her choosing.

It felt like a reprieve.

Vera knew that if she wanted him to consider renegotiating their open-relationship agreement, she needed him to be comfortable. He certainly wasn't comfortable right now.

"You have so many useful contacts," she said instead. "You know how helpful they were to me when I started out in this field."

And that was, at least, the truth. Peter Christoff had taken her under his wing, had introduced her to art experts at monied art galleries, and had convinced her to move in with him while she had still been in graduate school.

Life as interpreted by Peter Christoff was a heady experience indeed. The Christoffs lived a jet-setting lifestyle most people only dreamed about. It was a necessary part of Peter's business world. Peter's uncle was getting older and he need an heir to his small Ukrainian "business" empire, and Peter was in the running along with his two cousins, Uncle Ilya's sons.

She didn't know what sort of work they all did at the time they had met. Now she knew, that ever since they had begun living together, Peter had been struggling to establish himself as an independent diamond merchant. He tried as hard as he could to make a living in a business separate from his family's dealings and still maintain that certain level of carefree luxury.

"Verushka, you are not happy." Vera felt the bed dip as Peter, stripped out of his clothes and slid under the covers.

"No, I'm not." She took the opening he gave her. "When we got together, we were never exclusive, right?"

She felt him stiffen next to her as he replied. "No. We never were exclusive. We were free to enjoy one-time lovers, as long as we remained emotionally together."

"Peter, I know we have this don't-ask-don't-tell policy, but... I don't know if you realize I've never actually slept with anyone else."

He sighed. "Your other lover is your art, my love. Your career. We do spend time apart – weeks, sometimes." He shifted to look at her. "Are you seriously trying to tell me that in all this time... " He sighed. "You mean you never took anyone else to your bed?"

The little reading light was still on. She turned to him. The lines of Peter's face were illuminated in a baroque play of light and shadow, highlighting his sharp cheekbones, straight nose, and strong jaw. He was perfect – except for his zipper malfunction issues. "In our five years of marriage, I have never been with anyone else. That's not to say I didn't think about it, but... I'm different from you."

Her mind was drawn back to Aunt Yelena. She was like the mother Vera had always dreamt of. She raised Peter after her husband killed his parents in some kind of a blood feud. The details were never discussed in her presence, but the way in which Peter had become an adopted orphan was no secret within the family.

One didn't betray the clan, and one didn't leak business information in an effort to gain his own business financing. Peter was five when it all went down. Once he got old enough, Uncle Ilya explained these facts to him and tendered what apologies he could.

That's why Peter was driven to separate from the clan and stand on his own feet. She knew he did his best to keep his activities transparent to Uncle Ilya. It wouldn't do to infringe upon family operations.

His adoptive parents supported his effort wholeheartedly. When Peter had first brought Vera home, they'd welcomed her with open arms and open hearts. Only after she married Peter, however, did they feel comfortable discussing family business at the dinner table.

"Aunt Yelena was appalled when she found out I let you get away with what she calls 'your damn tomcatting'," Vera said. "She told me I deserve better."

"You told her?" There was surprise in Peter's voice, and no small amount of displeasure.

"She's the only person I can talk to about these things. Letting anyone else know would be too… humiliating." Her family hated Peter as it was, and her friends and colleagues looked up to her as the rising star in her field. Many of them received his generous help while forging professional contacts. Not for the first time did she wonder how many had slept with him as well.

She put her papers on the night table and turned her reading light off. Then she turned away and, despite the heavy tension in the air, she went to sleep.

They didn't kiss good-night.

CHAPTER 5

Peter was lying on his side of the bed. They had pushed the single, European style beds together when they moved in, but the mattresses still formed a gap between them and that gap formed a convenient barrier right now. Vera was turned away from him, pretending to sleep. Or sleeping – it was hard to tell anymore. She'd learned to fake sleep disturbingly well over the years. In all this time, she had never said anything negative about his lady friends. His needs had exceeded those of other men, and Vera would have been unable to fulfill them.

At least he never lied about it.

He loved his wife with all his heart. Intelligent, brave, creative and stubborn, she was everything the other women were not. The older she was, the more attractive she got and her stature in the international arts community continued to grow.

She wasn't just a mousy grad student who lacked confidence anymore. Nowadays she was Dr. Vera Christoff, a professor. An international authority on sub-Caucasian icons. She was a star, and her light was bright enough to bring him cheer on the darkest day. The sex bunnies he enjoyed were generally of the arm-candy variety, although he did maintain a stable of accomplished companions in his favorite ports of call. Whenever he saw a woman with a talent for something special, he exerted himself on her behalf whether he ended up sleeping with her or not.

He was a catalyst. He got people together – but only the right people – and then he sat back and watched things happen. Concerts, recordings, art exhibits. Business ventures, new inventions, financing for promising start-ups. He kept tabs on all his protégés, and when he was in town, they regaled him with stories of their success. Most of them also warmed his bed as a show of appreciation. Yet none of them were as brilliant, as enticing and as unpredictable as his wife.

Her breathing was regular now, and he detected a light snore. That made life a lot easier, because he had a date to keep, and as much as he trusted his wife with the generalities of family business matters, he didn't want to burden her with its ugly reality.

Against his wishes and his strenuous efforts, he was getting sucked back into its murky waters, and he hated every second of it.

This trip wasn't just about rescuing artwork at the dawn of war.

This trip was all business.

Uncle Ilya was the one who was supposed to be here right now carrying out the transaction as well as negotiating further shipments. The old man had taken ill, though, and neither one of his sons had ever bothered to learn the languages necessary for doing business in the region. Their Ukrainian was barely passable, and their Russian was even worse. Their high school Spanish was good only for hiring the *illegales* to do the landscaping for their lavish California homes.

Peter's watch alarm chimed. He silenced it and got out of bed. He hoped he was just imagining being so loud and fumbling. Even the slither of fabric against his skin sounded raucous in the night.

He closed his belt buckle and seated the gun holster in the small of his back. The semiautomatic was hot and loaded, with a round already in the chamber.

Carefully, he picked up his shoes and tiptoed to the door that led to the balcony. He had already decided to avoid his own bodyguards – they not only kept him safe, they also reported on his activities to the family. He resented being sucked back into the morass of international arms dealing, and he doubly hated the organization keeping tabs on him. He would work on his own, and pursue his own agenda. After years of unavoidable power plays, he was entirely done with answering to his babysitters.

The lock was already open from before. The old wooden door swung into the room with the slightest creak. Then he was out on the balcony, in the fresh air of the night. A solitary light from a nearby intersection almost reached the trellis. He'd climb by feel, then, pressed by his need to make his one o'clock meeting on time.

GINA WASN'T cold, because she was smart enough to bring the blanket from the top of her bed to the balcony and wrapped it around herself like a poncho.

She couldn't sleep. The whole situation with the Christoff's was taking an ugly turn. She couldn't bring herself to trust Peter's assertion that his wife, Vera, was okay with him sleeping around. She had heard of such relationships, of course, but who really did that? Peter Christoff was bullshitting her. She couldn't imagine otherwise.

Most of all, she didn't understand why a woman of Dr. Christoff's stature would demean herself by sharing her husband with all comers. The woman was brilliant, dedicated, and serious about the work she did. She may not have been a supermodel, but she sure wasn't ugly. Peter Christoff must have brought *something* of value into her life, but unless it was just a pretty smile and bodyguards, Gina failed to see it.

A SMALL CREAK informed her that her downstairs neighbor opened the door onto the balcony. She heard it close, and wondered if he or she also couldn't sleep. Then she wondered why. Gina shook the blanket off her shoulders, rose out of her chair, and tiptoed over to the waist-high wall. She leaned to peek down.

She stilled.

The silhouette looked familiar – much like Peter Christoff. He swung his leg over the masonry railing and took hold of the trellis that supported the ancient grapevines.

Peter doesn't seem to care for staircases.

She watched him descend until he disappeared in the dark. He never once looked up. Few minutes later she saw him peek both ways into the street and make a right.

Gina recalled the lucky telephone call that broke up their kiss.

The one o'clock meeting.

Peter would "be there," and "he had the goods."

There must have been a connection to the letter that let them through the Serbian checkpoint with such ease. She frowned, wondering what the goods might be.

Artwork?

His armed detail spoke of something more prosaic. After all, Peter Christoff seemed to know just about anyone.

Curiosity washed over her with frightful intensity, and along with it came that devil-on-one-shoulder voice that had enticed her into many an adventure.

The trellis beckoned. What's good for the gander is good for the goose, she thought quickly as she tried to suppress the memories of her occasional adventures that had threatened to take a bad turn in the past.

But Peter... Peter climbed right down, eschewing a perfectly good staircase.

The streets seemed as empty as the garden below.

Just a peek. A little peek.

Gina she scurried into her room, put on her sneakers, and pulled on a dark blue waterproof jacket. Peter Christoff was a man of many secrets. She didn't think she'd like any of them, but she certainly intended to find out more.

If the trellis had held Peter, it would hold her, too. She was probably lighter by a few pounds than he was – and going down a vine-covered wooden ladder, even in the dark, was a much easier climb than many of the cliff faces she had ascended without the benefit of a safety harness.

Gina let out a controlled exhale as she swung her leg over the railing and grasped the old wood in her hands. She found a crossbeam with her right toe, then with the left. Adrenaline buzzed in her veins just enough to give her that special, alert edge as she considered every move, every minute shift of her weight.

One floor down.

Two.

Three.

She groped her way in the dark, step by careful step. Soon she was level with what must have been Peter and Vera's room.

Step by step, with occasional fumbles in the dark, she reached and grasped and slipped until she felt the soft grass under her feet.

The little garden gate was still open from Peter's passage, and Gina felt relief wash over her because the metal hinges were probably old, and would probably have squeaked in the dark, had she tried to open it.

She slipped through.

The space behind the building was dark in the way of gardens that absorbed light this time of the night. She felt her way through the blades of old, uncut grass and over stone pavers, careful not to trip, until she felt firm stone underfoot and felt the texture of a stucco wall against her hand.

An alley?

She made her way to the intersection and peeked around the corner. Nobody.

The street was deserted and silent, and the cobblestones looked like waves under the sparse lights of the street lanterns. She didn't expect the sound of pounding blood in her ears. She turned right.

Walk as though you belong.

A distinct gate on a building across the street told her she was headed in the direction of the parked cars. The wrought ironwork and an old family crest had caught her eye from the back of the car many hours ago.

Reassured, she sped up. Whatever goods Peter had would probably be stored in the secure courtyard that Vera had mentioned earlier. They might even be in one of his three cars.

A courtyard, in these parts, meant a wall and a gate.

A problem, then – but not an unsurmountable one. She took a deep breath and kept walking.

THE BUILDINGS WERE glued together like swallow's nests, hugging the steep hillside in a gentle curve. Flat space was at a premium, and Gina wondered why the residents had built a secure parking lot in a town like this.

The locals parked their small, beat-up cars by the curb in front of their houses, yet not every house had a car in front of it. Just like in Italy, car ownership was expensive. Here, perhaps even more so.

She stopped and looked around. There was no sign of Peter.

The street was deserted, with its tall buildings looking down on her, scolding her. She felt that sudden, oppressive weight again, the knowledge that she was treading on ancient ground where blood had been spilt over and over in an eternal struggle for resources. The ghosts of the long-dead crowded over her shoulders.

This was nothing like the thrill of climbing a rock face.

Nor did she stumble under the pressure of centuries back in the US. America felt open and free and almost virgin. Few, if any, of her ancestors laid buried there, and the long-dead First Nations didn't come to mind nearly as much. The land was so vast, it was difficult to imagine its plains and mountains as densely crowded as Europe. In America she could breathe free. Here, she probably stood on some ancient battle ground with the spilled and long-dried blood paved many layers underfoot.

An image of layers upon layers of bones under her feet sprang to her mind as the wind stirred around her shoulders.

She shivered.

It felt as though the ghosts of the long-dead hissed in their long-dead tongues, disconsolate.

Standing still allowed her to look more closely at the facades of the buildings, and that's how she noticed that the seemingly impenetrable wall of buildings was punctuated by regularly appearing gates.

Where there was a gate, there might be a passageway.

As she pondered the thought, she heard the roar of a truck engine from afar. Startled, she jerked around to make sure she was still alone. She walked on, examining the still walls and their doors, and especially their gates.

Three houses later, she found a wall that had no windows. She would have passed it by, had she not been looking for something out of the ordinary. No windows meant no people. She looked up and felt satisfaction settle on her like a blanket, because this was not the wall of a building. It rose only ten feet up, and there was a gate few yards ahead. It was metal and seemed more modern than the others, and it stood open.

Gina walked up to the gate, step by a slow, steady step.

Every grain of grit under her feet grated against the pavement, eager to give her presence away. Her heart beat so loud, anyone could hear it miles away. She shut her mouth and focused on breathing through her nose, in and out, nice and deep and quiet.

The truck she heard before roared louder, and a car door closed on the other side of the wall.

Slowly, she retraced her steps and ducked into a deeper shadow that was cast by the building next to her. She felt safer now, less exposed, but she wanted to see what the goods were going to be.

Peter Christoff was dealing something, trading in something. She was wondering whether he was going to hawk some of the saved antiquities. There were so many – and he'd catalogued them with his wife before. He could've tampered with the records, and she would never know. The thought of such subterfuge made her stomach clench. She felt a driving need to get inside the courtyard and see for herself.

Her mind flitted back to their hotel. The front of that building had presented a similar, strong façade, yet the back had but a hip-high garden gate.

Barely enough to keep the chickens contained during the day.

If there were a trellis on the neighboring house, then she might be able to scale it and look over the wall.

Hugging the shadows, she took several more steps back. She dragged her fingertips over the pale stucco of the building – and released a breath of relief when the cool, stone surface gave way to weathered wood. The pads of her fingers slipped over the cracks between the planks, detecting the slight give and rasp of blistering paint.

The gate was old. It wasn't even locked.

She pressed on the lever that released the latch, and pushed the heavy wooden gate open.

The creak of its old hinges was probably negligible during the light of day, but its jarring sound made her jump. She slipped through the narrow gap and gently pushed the gate closed again.

She looked around.

The old, stucco walls flanked her to left and to right, meeting up in an arched ceiling that rose into the darkness above her. Gina felt a thrill rise inside her – this, then, was the passageway that led through the buildings. The silhouette of the passageway's other end was arched on top and rectangular on the bottom. The ambient light on the other side made the distance seem several car lengths away.

She bent her knees and spread her arms out for balance as she took her first halting steps in the dark. Smooth, uneven cobblestones rose and fell under her sneakers. *This is going well…*

She tripped. A bright, metallic clang reverberated through the passage as she almost fell in the dark.

Gina froze. No shouts, no sounds of alarm. She smelled the faint must of mildew that comes from storing things it dark places, and a whiff of motor oil.

The night remained still. Ever so slowly, she crouched, feeling her way around her obstacle. Small wheel, wire spokes, a hard seat. A bicycle? No, a small child's tricycle. Gina released the breath she didn't know she had been holding and continued to navigate her way around a cluster of bikes and trikes, stored lumber and what, in the dark, felt like car parts and gardening tools.

She escaped the cavernous confines of the passage with considerable relief. Her eyes, dilated from the darkness of the passage, had allowed her to see more than she expected. Her hearing became keen in the darkness as well. The truck that she had heard go down the street earlier on, the very truck that made her seek refuge and look for an alternate way to see into the courtyard, idled right next to the building under which she had just passed. Its bright lights illuminated the wall.

She saw an outline of a trellis covered with grapevines. She considered climbing up – yet if anyone looked up, she risked detection.

Gina looked around again and was surprised to find that the rear wall of the secure parking lot wasn't a masonry garden wall. The parking lot ran the length of the property and its rear boundary was demarcated by a tall, chain-link fence. Gina looked up. The fence was topped with concertina wire, and was transparent, yet the cars parked in the parking lot itself offered her cover.

She crept toward the fence, mindful of keeping her footfalls silent despite the cover of the of the truck's diesel engine rumble.

Few scraggly weeds climbed up the wire fencing. Their leaves were almost gone, and she hoped that the shape of the remaining ones would break the outline of her body if anyone happened to shine a light her way.

45

The truck shifted its gears. The sound changed. She froze.

Seconds dragged by as she choked on diesel fumes and adrenaline.

But she had to see.

She had to know.

She peeked out around the side of a parked car and the truck shifted gears again and moved back and forth in the small space, adjusting only to turn and pull all the way in. The truck looked like it was brand new, and it was the kind with shiny, metal sides that she used to see delivering merchandise on large highways. Seeing it in the city, let alone in a small town with narrow and antiquated roads, had been unexpected.

It gleamed in the dark, and its reflective surface also served to shed extra light on the area, reflecting the headlights of a nearby vehicle. As soon as the truck was all the way in, somebody shut the steel door, and the lights of the truck no longer aimed in her general direction.

She released the breath she didn't know she had been holding, and found a place to crouch down.

Voices.

Men. Two, or three?

Someone turned the truck engine off, filling the void between her and the men with dangerous silence. Two guys climbed down from the cab of the truck. She could see only parts of their bodies. Another man – Peter and Vera's driver – startled her into freezing stiff again as he peeled away from the shadows.

He approached them.

Greetings were exchanged.

She heard Peter Christoff's familiar baritone.

Four men, then.

They spoke Russian. Gina struggled to pick up even the gist of their conversation from far away. Frustrated, she nosed her way to the fence, between the two cars. A rectangular pile of some stored goods sat to the left of one of the cars. If she only could hide behind that pile, she could hear better.

She couldn't move one car over without risking detection. All she saw was the shiny surface of the truck, and people's feet.

The feet began to move closer.

"Do you have it?" One of the truckers asked.

"Yes," Peter replied.

"Which one?" The man asked again.

Peter's response was too fast for Gina to understand. She kept her eyes and ears open. Her heartbeat was so loud, she could hardly hear over it and almost felt the very sound of it would give her away.

She was stuck crouching behind this fence now.

I wish I could go back.

This had been a terrible idea, spying on a man who travelled with armed guards in what was surely going to become a war zone. She knew she just had to hold still and not move, though, because movement and noise would give her away.

An unmistakable hiss of a match being struck disturbed the sudden silence, and she soon smelled the acrid odor of cheap tobacco.

"Good," the other man said. "I have what you asked for. Let's see them now!"

"A moment, please."

The crunching of grit underfoot and his familiar baritone informed Gina that Peter moved away. A trunk popped open.

Of one of their black vehicles?

If so, she didn't know which one, and furthermore, she wondered why would a buyer of antiquities bring a large tractor trailer.

She peeked around the fender of the car, just enough to be able to see. Even though she couldn't see the men directly, the reflective surface of the truck's container space provided a somewhat distorted picture of what was going on.

Her heart leapt in excitement.

Something. Anything.

Another parked car's lights went on to illuminate the car Peter just opened. The reflection showed on the shiny wall of the truck like on a funhouse mirror.

It was the best Gina could do.

She watched Peter Christoff's reflection as he pulled a long, heavy crate out of the large trunk. The other men came closer. One produced a strong knife and pried the wooden lid open. Peter anchored the crate against his hip as he pulled the long cylinder out. It looked familiar, with a pointed tip at one end and small wings in the back.

47

"Ah, a Stinger! Good man!" The truck driver's laughter spoke of appreciation and pleasure.

Gina understood the words just right. But a "stinger," an English word inserted into a Russian conversation, could mean many things.

"How many?" Gina understood that, too. It occurred to her that his Russian might be as rudimentary as hers, and that he and Peter were using it only as a language of convenience.

"Five," Peter replied. His distorted reflection waved at the trunk of the car. The two men pulled out five long crates out and carried them into the cab of the truck, one by one. Gina watched them stack the pale, wooden crates in the back of the cab. She couldn't tell for sure, but the crates seemed to have a series of numbers printed on the outside. A sudden image from a newscast came to her mind.

Stinger missiles?

Weapons weren't her line of expertise, but even she recalled seeing them on the news after their success in the Gulf War. In her mind, they were linked to destructive power and precision. They also looked smaller in real life than she expected them to be. It seemed hardly possible that such a small, elegant rocket could down a helicopter or an airplane.

Her throat soured when she reevaluated the situation: Peter Christoff was dealing weapons to a foreign national, and the deal didn't look official.

"How many more can you get?" The truck driver asked.

"How much money do you have?" Peter asked. Their laughter was drowned out by the sound of a ramp that fell from the back of the truck. Soon, a sound of a new, smaller engine broke the night. Gina was amazed to see an orange forklift back out of the truck and navigate down the steel ramp. It carried a palette of long, narrow boxes. They were dark and looked weathered, but despite it all, Gina saw an imprint of numbers and Cyrillic characters on their side. The passenger from the truck moved five heavy crates to the rear of the parking lot, and all four men worked to cover the load with an old tarp. Their conversation was obscured by the sounds of machinery and by the rustling of the old tarp. Gina was able to pick up only a few words and fragments. The ones that stuck in her head were the phrases "This will work better" and "We have more," and "Arr-peh-geh."

CHAPTER 6

Gina felt like three hours had passed, even though it was likely less than half an hour. Even so, a half-hour of crouching behind a fence left her muscles stiff. Blood circulation to her feet was getting cut off from squatting, judging from the way her feet tingled. It felt like having ants trapped right under her skin.

She didn't dare move.

The two truckers backed their tractor trailer out of the courtyard and Peter and his driver walked out to the gate. She heard Peter say good-night. His driver's shift wasn't over yet, though, and he stayed. This vexed Gina, because she wanted to have a closer look at the series of symbols on the crates that now sat under the tarp. If Peter was giving Stinger missiles to these guys, it stood to reason that he was getting something of value back from them. He wasn't being paid in cash. Not yet, anyhow.

Horse-trading deals were not uncommon in the art world. Gina had heard of them, and had even seen one, but she never had a reason to consider how principles of market demand and enlightened self-interest applied to international arms deals. Peter Christoff might have been doing a good deed by saving precious artifacts from the ravages of impending civil war, but in Gina's eyes, he no longer walked on the side of the angels.

As Gina tried to think the situation through, she eased her butt to the ground and stretched her legs out. She grimaced with pain as blood began to rush back to her feet, and breathed as quietly as possible. It would take five minutes before she could walk normally, and she'd like to give Peter another ten minute head start.

THE BALCONIES of the hotel rooms were like dark eyes, hooded and brooding, with the window like fathomless irises of an ancient creature.

Gina stopped in her tracks.

No telling who was watching her.

For the first time in years of adventure-seeking thrills, she was scared, yes, but fear was not an insurmountable obstacle. She pushed herself to reason it all out as she observed the building and the garden behind it.

The arms deal freaked me out.

It's dark. Everything looks different at night.

Stay rational. Keep breathing.

The little garden gate was now closed. Perhaps Peter had closed it as he came back. She wondered why he hadn't taken the front door and the staircase to begin with.

She scrutinized the balconies. They seemed abandoned. Now that she knew what she should not have known, climbing back to her room seemed more dangerous than it had been to scramble down the trellis to follow Peter. Taking the front door was out of question because of the bodyguards and their rotations.

Gina took a deep breath and let it out bit by bit. She eased the garden gate open and endured the squeak of its metal hinges, closed it, and took cover by the wall. She looked up – there was no way she would know if anyone was on the balcony. As quietly as she could, she grasped the leafless, gnarly vines and the rough wood of the lattice.

She began to climb. It felt like forever. Passing by Peter and Vera's balcony was fraught with hazard. She only hoped he would not be out there, sitting in the dark, only to hear her rustle and creak on her way up.

TEN MINUTES later, Gina shucked her clothes off, pulled on her cotton pants and a T-shirt, and crawled into her bed. Questions spun in her head, all tangled and yearning for order, but she knew there was little hope to make sense of it all now. She tossed and turned in bed while dark possibilities churned on.

At two-thirty, she still couldn't stop the turbulent flow of her mind. Finally she forced herself to lie on her back and count her exhales. The theory was to count from one to ten, over and over again, until she felt asleep. By three, she caught herself thinking of the sleek, black Stinger missile, and had to start counting at one again.

One, two, three, four...

Her brother Tony had been injured in the line of duty by stolen US ordnance. It cost him his arm and a lot more besides. But this wasn't the time to think of this, of stolen Stinger missiles in the hands of unknown men who used Russian only as a language of convenience. This wasn't the time to think of people writhing in pain, crying out, dying.

One, two, three...

This wasn't the hour to dwell on depressed, mutilated soldiers whose health and future was ended with a weapon stolen, bought on the black market, turned against them. Nor was it time to recall Tony's suicide attempt.

One, two, three...

She didn't get past five when she got lost in endless speculation as to how the missiles were stolen. Which base? Gina uttered a soft curse and resumed her breathing. She had to start at one again, all too aware that her digital watch alarm was set for eight. She would try to solve the problems of the world when she woke up.

BREAKFAST wasn't going well for Vera. She hadn't slept well, and judging from the circles under Peter's eyes, neither had he. She wished she'd had the courage to initiate 'the conversation' years ago, as soon as it became apparent that their open-marriage arrangement was only to Peter's benefit. She stirred her coffee for maybe the fifth time, took a deep breath, and fixed her eyes on her husband. "Peter, we really should…" she said.

"Good morning!" Gina stood at the door. To Vera's experienced eye, she looked as tired as Peter did. Well, no wonder. They shouldn't have stayed up.

"Good morning, Gina," Vera said and sipped more coffee. If she made a face, she could blame it on the off-brand instant. "There's breakfast," she pointed to the buffet. "Help yourself."

"Thank you," Gina said, but her smile was forced. Something was, obviously, on the younger woman's mind. Vera hoped it was a profound sense of guilt. She hadn't staked out her own territory regarding Peter, that much was true. She had been watching his expert attempts to bond and influence another 'brilliant young mind' with her customary, bemused smile. They had their arrangement. He wasn't stepping out, exactly. Vera would have felt humiliated to complain. Instead, she raised her head up high and strove to save face. Peter's Aunt Yelena had that tough old bird carriage, and Vera imitated her, well aware of her actions.

"Did you sleep well?" Vera asked.

"Not very, I'm afraid," Gina said, and the truthfulness of her response was corroborated by the deep circles under her eyes.

"Sorry to hear that," Vera said as she stood up and stretched. "Me neither." She eyed Gina with covert interest. If Gina admitted to a bad night, maybe it meant that Peter failed to satisfy her. The thought mollified her some. "We'll need to catalogue the last crate of artifacts before we leave. And you did want to walk around the square and look around, didn't you? You have to see the church. It has lovely frescoes that go way back."

PETER LINGERED over breakfast just long enough to let Gina and his wife finish their meal and leave. The unmistakable signs of jealousy that he had just seen Vera display had been getting worse over time.

Her attitude confused him. He'd given her everything - money, opportunities, contacts. He loved her, and was quite sure that she was aware of that. He had never felt that depth of emotion for anyone. They had their arrangement, one that dated back to before they were married, where they were both free to sleep around as long as they remained each other's primary emotional love interest.

Peter had never asked if Vera made use of her freedom. He didn't want to know. Jealously would have reared its ugly head then, and Peter didn't want to be a hypocrite. It came as quite a shock to him, then, to hear Vera say that she had never taken a lover. Not even when she could have – the interest of her colleagues was unmistakable.

He didn't understand why not.

He could, and did. She could, yet chose not to. If Vera agreed to something she later regretted, she should have said so right away. The days when she looked up to him with endless devotion in her eyes were, apparently, over. The friendship and respect he still felt were tainted by a kind of hurt he didn't understand. They had their deal. If she had a problem with it, why the hell didn't she speak up?

He sipped the last dregs of his coffee. It mirrored his feeling perfectly. It was as bitter as resentment, and its temperature reminded him of fear.

GINA WALKED by Dr. Christoff's side down a familiar street. The stone edifices of old buildings looked less foreboding in the light of the day, and most of the parked cars were gone. She forced herself to not look at the old, weathered gate where she'd slipped through the passage yesterday. Instead, she let her eyes absorb the clean, Mediterranean lines of the buildings on the other side of the street. They only seemed shorter, because they were built downhill. Their whitewash gleamed even in the pale autumn sun, and the red terracotta roofs added the color that was, by now, gone from the window boxes.

"I thought it would be better to catalogue all those items here, away from prying eyes. No need to bring the artifacts to the hotel," Vera said as they approached the steel gate. She pushed a button and smiled at the wall, and the door opened almost right away. Gina studied the wall with casual interest. There must have been a camera somewhere – but where? And was there a camera by the rear fence, too?

She'd been lucky the night before. For the first time in her life, she had thought back to potential disasters instead of just relishing in her latest thrilling conquest. She had taken a foolish risk. She could have fallen, the trellis could have broken, she could have been mugged, she could have been discovered and captured – and all that in a foreign country with a war going on where she didn't even speak the most common languages. She shuddered.

"Are you feeling all right?" Vera stopped and squinted against the morning sun at her. Gina felt her look of solicitous concern and felt an immediate sense of relief. She was glad, now, that she hadn't yielded to temptation and slept with Peter. She was not one of those 'other women' Vera barely tolerated. No, she was a student, and would become a colleague someday.

"I'm fine. Just tired. I think it's the uncertainty of this whole trip. Thank you for bailing me out – "

"You don't have to keep thanking me," Vera said dryly. "Had it not been me, my husband would've positively insisted that you come along." The bitter note in Vera's voice reminded Gina of rancid olive oil. That, and dust. It grated between the teeth.

It appeared that Vera assumed that Gina had actually slept with Peter. Gina bit back her retort that 'nothing happened.' Kissing wasn't nothing, and if she opened that can of worms, she would then have to explain about the kiss, and how things would've been different, had it not been for an inopportune telephone call.

She applied herself to work, filling out forms and taking photographs of each cross, icon, and censer with diligent dedication. She didn't feel comfortable clearing the air, and she did feel a measure of guilt, and for that she would atone by doing the best job ever.

THE ARTIFACTS were registered, photographed, and classified. Vera took in Gina's contrite expression and the bent angle of her head as she filled out yet another form. The girl was talented and capable. Under different circumstances, Vera would have been happy to become her mentor. She would teach her, guide her, introduce her to the auction house managers and gallery owners and museum curators. She would have done all that, had Gina not slept with her… husband.

The situation had a *déjà vu* feel to it, and Vera's thoughts wandered to the promenade of young, talented women that had populated Peter's bed over the five years of their marriage. Many of them were more than just a pretty face. They had talents and skills, and had they not yielded to Peter's persuasive attentions, Vera would have befriended them, guided them.

Only then did it occur to her that Peter was stealing not only her dignity and sense of inner balance, but potential students and friends as well. Her eyes rested on a tendril of brown hair that escaped from Gina's ponytail. She was quite lovely. The long neck and large eyes, the aquiline nose – she would sculpt well.

The thought made her pause. When Vera was not an art historian and a philanthropist, she was primarily a painter. Her connection to three-dimensional form barely fulfilled graduation requirements. She didn't know why she felt like sculpting right now, but the bittersweet pressure that always drove her to the canvas had been building up for quite a while now. This time, the outlet of her creative angst wanted to be set in stone.

She filed the thought away and turned her attention to a large cardboard file box. It contained the catalogue of the collected artifacts, but more importantly, it contained the associated letters from abbots and priests who entrusted her with church property.

The box looked vulnerable. There was no way to make copies of all this mess, not in this backwater little town. She watched Gina put a new roll of film in her camera. Of course. The solution was so obvious, it couldn't be even called a flash of inspiration.

"I have a favor to ask of you," Vera said.

GINA LIFTED her head. "Yes?"

"This documentation – this is all there is right now. I told you before that the artifacts will be stored in a museum in Vienna, where a friend of mine works as a curator. However," Vera paused, trying to formulate her words in the least damaging way. "The art world can be incredibly political. You have heard of all the stored artwork that was appropriated after World War II, right?"

Gina nodded. "Yes. In fact, certain Etruscan artifacts were returned to Italy in the seventies, and they contained the Greek red-face pottery. I remember reading about that."

"Yes. So, I want to prevent a similar situation from even occurring. In case my friend loses his position, I don't want the new powers-that-be decide to just appropriate these items. They're meant to remain in storage for the duration of the war, but that's all. I have a proof of their provenance in here," and she jutted her chin toward the files, "and I have a proof that they were given up to us voluntarily, and for safekeeping only. These papers are extremely important. Unfortunately, they're the only copies we have."

Gina understood immediately. "You want me to take pictures of the documentation," she said. It made so much sense. She was so happy to do this. It was, after all, for Dr. Christoff. The woman was a legend in her field. "Sure, I'll be happy to do that. So, how many pictures do you want me to take?"

"How much film do you have?"

IT TOOK FIVE out of her remaining six rolls of film, but they spread the papers out into neat groupings and Gina jury-rigged a tripod and took the photos from above.

"That's all, then," she said.

"If we wrap things up here, we could walk over to town and have a nice lunch." Vera said. "The tobacco shop might have film and batteries. There were also those frescoes I wanted to show you." She looked at her younger companion. Gina would never become her protégé, but she was proving to be an invaluable helper.

CHAPTER 7

PETER LOOKED up as the front door swung open. Vera and Gina burst through, cursing and laughing and drenched like wet dogs. The sight drew a smile to his face, which was why he was stuck with a goofy grin when the two wiped water out of their eyes and noticed him.

"I suppose you think this is funny, Peter Christoff," Vera said, but not in a mean voice.

"I just love to hear you laugh." There was undeniable truth in that. She was beautiful when she laughed, and he realized that she did that too seldom of late, and that he missed it.

He stood and made his way to them over the suddenly slick floor. "You two need a hot bath. I'll have them send tea upstairs. Would you like anything else?"

"Cookies!" Gina said with a grin. Getting soaked this time of the year was never a lot of fun, but then again, she enjoyed Peter's version of the welcoming committee. She turned to Vera. "Is he always such a gentleman?"

"It's his best feature," Vera said after a short pause. "Of course, he has his share of flaws, but all in all, he can be extremely charming and considerate. Even dangerously so."

Peter stiffened a bit at the back-handed praise. Still, she was laughing, and Gina got over whatever had been bugging her earlier. He should have expected Gina to be upset this morning – after all, he'd inflated her expectations, only to walk out on her because his shipment came in.

He resolved to try and make it up to her, and likewise, he resolved not to hurt Vera over it. He still didn't know what had changed between them, and since it wasn't something he could affect, he shoved the whole problem into the dustiest recess of his mind.

"May I?" He asked as he took Vera's soaked jacket. "You must be chilled. Go, have your bath. That's two teas and cookies, coming up!"

Peter watched as the women departed up the wide staircase before he placed the order with the kitchen. Then he settled in the wingback chair by the front window and stared at the downpour outside. They were supposed to be out of this little mountain town by dinnertime, except Peter had five crates of old Soviet RPG's to unload and his new contact was late in coming. His Bosnian buyer might have had mechanical trouble, or the sudden hard rain might have washed out the road.

Peter had provided fake ID for Ajax. There shouldn't have been any trouble at the Serbian checkpoint. He was sitting down here, close to the telephone, waiting for the word. The sooner those crates were out of the secure parking courtyard, the better.

GINA HISSED AS she lowered herself into the hot bath. She relished these ancient, claw foot bathtubs with their hand-held shower and no shower curtain. It felt very old-fashioned and comforting. Peter Christoff was right when he said she and Vera were chilled. Gina's jeans, jacket, and her long-sleeve shirt were all soaked, and so were her sneakers. Vera arranged for their clothes to be dried in the hotel's laundry, which left Gina with a pair of shorts and her long, cotton pajama pants. Traveling light had its disadvantages.

She reached for her orange-scented shortbread cookie and a cup of hot tea. The warmth and the sweetness commingled, and the bathroom was so foggy, the old glass tiles were matte with condensation. Gina closed her eyes in bliss. This was heaven, right here, with the wet heat permeating her stiff muscles. She noted how the physical pleasure of the bath even washed away her worry over the smuggled missiles, and the shipment of five pallets of something of equivalent value.

Then she realized she was thinking of it again.

The cookie turned to dust in her mouth, the air of the unvented bath became heavy and stifling, and her wet shoulders grew goosebumps.

Her reaction irritated her. She cleansed her palate with more tea and got out. Her perfectly warm and fabulous hot bath had been ruined by Peter Christoff's business.

"WHAT DO you mean, we're staying?" Vera asked. Her unmistakable alarm would, Peter knew, soon translate to a curious cat impersonation. Peter steeled himself against a regular inquisition.

He could lie.

He could prevaricate.

He could also distract. There was no reason for his lovely, artistic and erudite wife to worry over an obscure deal that was struck by Uncle Ilya. Hell, Peter himself didn't understand all the implications of it. His uncle told him all he needed to know. That did not include all he wanted to know.

"I got a call. I'm babysitting a shipment of goods, and the guy who's picking 'em up broke his axle on a rutted road. The regular road got flooded." He came up for breath. "You know – mountains. He can't make it until tomorrow at noon."

He watched the way Vera dried her shoulders and her arms, and when time came to dry her back, he stepped behind her and took the towel from her hands. "Here… let me help you." He rubbed down the hard-to-reach place between her shoulder blades, and continued down the smooth curve of her back. Her hips flared under the towel he held, and he had to remind himself what he'd been trying to do.

"You're so beautiful." She froze a bit, and he steeled himself for a sharp retort.

It never came. Her neck softened as she allowed her head to tilt to the side. The expanse of milk skin was marred by a round scar with jagged edges.

He brushed his lips against the place where the bullet had exited her body only two years ago. An old guilt resurfaced and threatened to spoil the moment. He pushed back against it hard, and moved onto the soft and unblemished area of her neck that didn't bear witness to the way he had failed to protect her back in Kiev.

He forced himself to focus on the here and now. When he brushed his lips against the soft skin that was still moist from the bath, he felt her melt against his chest as tension drained out of her frame

"Maybe being stuck here isn't as bad as all that," she whispered.

"Not bad at all," he murmured into her hair. "Here, come to bed so you don't catch a chill."

And she did.

GINA WAS on her way up the stairs, headed back from the downstairs utility area, where she had picked up her and Vera's dry clothing. She folded the garments and separated them into two piles. It was getting close to dinnertime and, figuring that Vera would want her black trousers back, Gina stopped by Peter and Vera's room. She knocked on their door.

Peter replied in what she had since learned was Serbian. Gina heard a bit of fumbling from the other side of the door before he opened just a crack. He peered out. His right arm was hanging down by his body. She glimpsed the dark contours of a gun. His hair was disheveled and his eyes looked glazed with sleep.

"I am sorry to disturb you," Gina said in her most neutral voice. "I was picking up the clothing from the dryer, and here are Vera's things." She extended the small pile toward the crack in the door.

"Thank you." Peter shot a cautious look up and down the hallway before he opened the door further to take the clothing with his right hand, which is how Gina caught an inadvertent glimpse of the slept-in bed and Peter's wife, who was still in it.

"Say… " his voice turned to a conspiratorial whisper. "Would you mind taking dinner on your own today? I'd like to take Vera out. Like a date."

"Oh! No, not at all." Gina found she was whispering back. "That's totally fine. You need some time alone. I can explore by myself, no problem."

"Let me give you a few extra dinars," Peter said. "You'll want to check out this coffee shop on the square. They have fabulous desserts. They're open late, too." As he turned to set Vera's clothing down and retrieve his wallet from a pile of papers that sat on the desk by the door, Gina spotted a familiar rectangle of creamy paper. It was the letter that Peter used to get them through the Serbian checkpoint. Her breathing quickened and she dropped her eyes to the floor.

"No, that's okay. I still have some cash."

"Bullshit," he hissed. "Your money's stuck in Dubrovnik, and Dubrovnik's under siege. It's lucky you have your passport with you. Here… take this." He waved her attempt at objections aside. "No, I absolutely insist."

Gina didn't even have a chance to change her mind and say a proper thank-you. She just stood there with a fistful of foreign currency. Peter Christoff had shut the door right in her face.

THE CHRISTOFF'S left their room half an hour later.

Gina heard them go, and as she sat on her bed, conflicting impulses warred in her chest. Peter was a mystery. His command of several languages, his armed body guards… his letter of passage.

And it might even hint at the nature of his international arms dealing.

She wanted to know what that letter said, and she wanted it bad enough, it hurt.

On the other hand, she wasn't suicidal. Despite Vera's professional fame and her benevolence toward Gina, and despite Peter's courtesy toward anything cute and female, Gina had no doubt in her mind that if she was caught snooping around, there'd be hell to pay.

She needed an excuse. Not for Peter or Vera – they would be gone for a while – but for the guards.

Thinking quickly, Gina dove into her duffle bag, dug up her spare bra, and stuffed in into her pants' pocket.

If any of the guards caught her, she'd plead her utter embarrasment and claim she came to retrieve her bra.

Hopefully, they'd try to protect Peter.

Hopefully, she'd escape unscathed.

As she peeked out her own door cracked open to make sure they walked all the way down the stairs and out of the building, a familiar surge of excitement built up in her chest. She walked to their door, and knocked on it.

Nobody replied.

Good – Gina was afraid they might leave a bodyguard behind. The coast was clear, however, so she looked up and down the hall with the same furtive look that she had seen Peter use earlier, and tried the door handle.

Locked.

It wasn't the kind of a lock she could pop open with a credit card, which was the extent of her burglary skills. There was no way to ask for a duplicate key without attracting attention, and the duplicate keys were guarded by the front desk attendant at all times.

The curious hunger that possesed her soul grew, and she couldn't shake it off. She wanted to see what was in that letter, because that letter just might guide her toward the buyer of the missiles. She was sure of it.

Finding out more wasn't just a trivial whim – it was personal. Tony had come back from his Mogadishu deployment with his arm in pieces. Worse, her brother didn't think like he could ever win again. Not if the rebels kept buying American or NATO armaments from the scum who leaked them from the bases for a quick profit. Somebody was pouring oil on the fire of discord, and Tony had been only one of many who have paid a heavy price.

Peter Christoff might be a nice and generous guy who offered her a ride out of a war zone,

GINA SPENT ten minutes sitting on her bed, dressed in her jeans. She pulled a stick of Wrigley's gum out of her last gum packet, unwrapped it, and proceeded to chew. When the gum was soft enough to be tacky,

Gina wrapped it in its foil again and set it aside. Then she moved onto the next stick, and the next, until all five pieces were turned into sticky, fragrant blobs. They didn't look like much, wrapped in their pieces of foil like lumpy little beads. She smiled, but her feelings were grim. Gina liked to think of herself as a good person, a law-abiding citizen of the world. Yet, the way she saw it, she didn't have much of a choice. She stowed the chewed gum in the left pocket of her jeans, slung her camera around her neck, and stepped out onto her balcony.

I can't believe I'm doing this.

This is so insane.

This is so awesome.

She checked her omnipresent camera, then slung it around her neck. Once a far-away pedestrian disappeared around a corner of their alley, she grasped the now-familiar trellis, and swung her leg over the side.

THE CLIMB down should have been easier the second time, yet she felt as though her heart would explode in her chest. Suppose somebody caught her – then what? She didn't have a good excuse, other than "getting my bra" and "getting lost."

Not good.

Once again she stemmed the flow of negative thoughts and forced herself to focus on her goal.

She wanted to know about that letter.

Only the glass-paned door separated her from satisfying her curiosity. The door was locked, just as she predicted it would be. As she had been sitting in her room, one floor up, chewing her gum, she had gone over the whole adventure step by step. She didn't dare break the glass pane open, not only because of the noise, but also because Peter and Vera would have noticed the cold winter air drafting in.

A quick scramble down the trellis, and she was standing on Peter and Vera's balcony with a pocket full of chewed gum. Their windows were dark. She peeked in through the glass, but didn't see anything.

She stepped up to the glass door and examined the panes in the waning light. Then she pulled her Swiss Army knife out of her right pocket and selected the smaller blade. It was the thinner one of the two, and as such, it cut through the paint and slid between the lattice of the door's framework and the thin length of wood that held the pane in its place. She ran her knife along all four sides. Then she slipped it between the caulk and the glass and twisted the blade a few times. After a soft creak, she watched in satisfaction as her knife pried the supporting structure away from the glass pane. She removed the delicate wooden rectangle, then she popped out the pane of glass. She set them both against the wall, upright, and reasonably secure. Gina's hand fit through the opening and she was able to reach the key in the lock. She turned it. There – a loud click, a clack as she pressed her hand onto the lever that the Europeans preferred over the American door knob.

She pulled – and the door swung open. She would have whooped for joy under ordinary circumstances. Now she only smiled and slipped inside.

THE LETTER was still there. After a brief thought, she risked turning the light on. She peered at the letterhead – something official. She tried to make out the Serbian Cyrillic text, but to no avail. Her Russian didn't transfer for her, at least not as easily as she thought it should have. Not all was lost, though. She still had two more exposures on her last roll of film. It was the same roll that contained much of the information for Vera's artifacts, and that was highly inconvenient but could not be helped. Gina set up the letter on the desk and aimed her camera at it. Focusing, a familiar task, took forever as her hands shook with nervous tension. Mint and bile mixed in the back of her throat.

Before she managed to click, a sound of footsteps broke the silence.

Somebody tried the door handle.

Gina froze.

Slowly, breathing as silently as she could, she backed out onto the balcony, smacked two blobs of still-soft gum onto the frame, and pressed the glass onto it. It should hold.

She glanced inside Peter and Vera's room.

Someone was trying to open the door.

She swung herself onto the trellis and scurried up to her own balcony, gasping like she was running a marathon. She failed to even take a picture. And, dammit, she left the light on. And she left the gum behind.

Once Gina got back to her room and made sure both of her doors were locked, she forced herself to steady her breathing and think again. She packed her camera away.

She needed a solid alibi – but that wasn't too hard. Now all she had to do was hurry outside and buy herself dinner and dessert with Peter's money. He would want to know how she spent her evening, and she had to sample not only a bit of local cuisine, but also at least one dessert in that coffee shop.

On her way down the stairs, she risked a glance toward Peter and Vera's door. The small hallway was deserted. She wondered who had disturbed her, and why.

66

CHAPTER 8

Stressed and hurried, Vera crinkled her nose at the odor of the hotel's coffee and sickly-sweet pastries that wafted from the kitchen. She humped their two suitcases down the stairs, step by resentful step. It occurred to her, not for the first time, that Peter and his henchmen were conveniently absent every time she needed them to fetch and carry.

And now she felt rushed, and torqued enough to make her stomach roil.

She really wanted to do one more walk-through of the city square, but time was of the essence. She suspected that she'd have barely enough time to choke down a piece of dry toast before the cars roared up to the hotel entrance.

Their little convoy had been scheduled to leave the town at dawn, but there had been a delay and Peter told her to be ready and on stand-by. Vera had packed up for both of them and made her way downstairs early, only to find Gina was already seated behind a table in the corner. She was hunched over her green, spiral-bound notebook.

"Good morning," Vera said.

She watched Gina jolt her head up. Her smile was a bit thin as she put her writing away. "Good morning to you too. Did you have a lovely dinner last night?"

"Yes," Vera said after a brief consideration. "Peter took me to a small, local place. He has a talent for finding the best under the most trying circumstances." She waved the waiter over for a cup of coffee, and helped herself to a boiled egg the consistency of a rubber ball. She considered a pastry. The fruit filling, which seemed cloying only minutes ago, was now attractive enough to make the egg palatable. "So how did you fare last night?" Vera said as she settled down across from Gina.

She watched the younger woman brush a nonexistent strand of hair off her cheek and tuck it behind her ear. There were circles under her eyes and she failed to suppress a yawn. "Peter was kind enough to point me in the right direction and front me some money for dinner." She flashed an embarrassed smile. "I had goat stew and bread for dinner, and then I walked over to that little sweet shop and made a pig of myself. And I had to have coffee with that, of course, except they didn't have any decaf, so I ended up staying awake until two."

Vera had a clock running in the back of her mind, and that clock told her that Peter was with her till late and never left, and therefore Gina's fatigue had nothing to do with her husband. Her expression softened as she laughed. "Oh, you discovered the culinary crossroads of Europe! Old-world desserts form Vienna and Budapest appear side by side with baklava and stuffed dates. Well, that's the Balkans for you. You won't find that anywhere else." She frowned at her food. "These hotel breakfasts are all the same after a while, though." She nudged her food with her finger. "Too bad I even asked."

"Too bad I answered," Gina said. "We could go over and pick something up before we leave, if you'd like."

"No. I was told we are to stay here and wait. We are leaving as soon as the guys come back." Vera sounded as vexed as she felt. These art exploration trips, despite their educational and philanthropic value, had begun to wear thin on her two years ago.

Right after she began to tire of it all, she discovered that having bodyguards was no guarantee against personal harm. Peter did his best to pull out of his family's wheelings and dealings for real after *that* unfortunate incident, and he almost succeeded in setting himself up as an independent diamond dealer as Vera's gunshot wound healed up.

They had lived in relative tranquility for almost a year. They spent more time together, and even Peter's tomcatting became exceptionally rare. His manner toward her had changed. Vera was now a precious jewel he almost lost. The change in their dynamic was eye-opening. Now that Vera knew what she had been missing, she worked harder than ever – not just for her own sake, but to impress Peter as well.

And Peter always came through with a backrub that kept her back from seizing up after a long painting session, or with a contact to display her new and as of yet unknown work to its fullest advantage.

Just as their lives fell into a comfortable groove, Uncle Ilya got sick. He was old and tough and experienced, and he was the one who structured the family deals and carried them out. He thought he'd never stop, not until Oleg became more experienced and Alexi learned to keep his temper on a leash. Yet there isn't much one can do about leukemia. Travel exhausted him. Other people's germs endangered him. His own sons lacked the language skills to do his job. The family needed help.

Peter could have said no. He didn't, though, because despite the fact that Uncle Ilya killed Peter's father all those years ago, he was still the closest thing to a father that Peter had ever had. Uncle Ilya backed Peter's early business ventures and he taught him how to do business clean. Vera had always thought that boosting Peter was a penance of sorts, a way to make up for what Ilya had considered to be a necessary murder all those years ago. And even had it not been for their tangled past, the Christoffs were a clan, and loyalty ran deep. Despite their internal feuds and power plays, the Christoff family always presented a united front to the outside world. Vera knew that Peter felt as obliged to Uncle Ilya as Ilya Christoff felt obliged to him.

"SOMETHING'S on your mind." Gina's voice interrupted her ruminations.

If you only knew.

"There is something on my mind all the time," Vera quipped and produced a smile. "This is a very tiring trip for all of us. Nobody expected the war to break out this soon. I thought we had at least until after Christmas, maybe even until spring. By then, there was a chance that all these issues could be resolved without resorting to full-out mobilization. They did so well at the Sarajevo Olympics - we all had high hopes back then. But… again, that's the Balkans for you. It's complicated."

"Sure," Gina said. "So... that shipment Peter's babysitting, what's his line of business, anyway?"

Vera peered at the younger woman over the rim of her coffee cup. "My husband is a diamond merchant. The Balkans have been not only a cultural crossroads, but also a trade center. I suspect he'll look to salvage what he can of his contacts here."

There was more. Vera knew that there was a lot more, in fact, but she didn't know whether Peter knew that she knew. To his credit, he did try to shelter her from Uncle Ilya's international arms business. Ilya's wife Yelena had no such reservations, however, and she had been doing her best to educate Peter's young bride about the things a woman in her position was likely to need. Yelena had meant well. She revealed management strategies that had helped her hold the family together as a cohesive whole. She explained the structures, the contacts, the goods. There was a pricing strategy just like in any other business, and there was the reality that Peter was going to be sucked right into it.

That's what made the last year so hard. Peter was under a lot of stress, and that stress sent him right back to his old comfort zone: his playboy days.

She could just taste his craving for external validation in the air, and at those times, she watched his eyes follow other women. Later, traces of their perfume grew bitter as she tasted them on his skin. Dealing diamonds was a lot easier for him - a bad diamond deal would only cost him money.

No need for covert night-time shipments and armed guards.

They could manage on Vera's slim academic earnings if they had to, but they never had to. Now, though, it wasn't just money that could be lost if the deal went south. Now they dealt in lives, both their own and those of all that participated in whatever conflict Uncle Ilya decided to fuel. There was a dark side, a bloody side that became all too apparent when the bodyguards showed up again. That was almost one year ago – and almost one year ago, Peter began to relieve himself of the extra stress with his arm candy again.

Vera tried not to mind. It should have been the same as when they met, or when they married. They still had their deal – except now Vera knew the comfort and joy of being the "only one." The special one. The one Peter strove to keep just for himself.

70

If it only were that easy.

She sighed and finished the coffee that had grown bitter and cold in her cup once again.

PETER STRETCHED his legs toward Hotel Adria, knowing this would be his last opportunity for exercise until they stopped for the night. The crew that came to pick up the old, Soviet-era RPGs had been running late, and they'd had trouble loading up because they didn't have a forklift. Peter and his shadows all had to pitch in, unloading the individual boxes of the pallets and stacking them in the bed of a noisy construction dump truck. It was the only truck big enough the Bosnians could find, and it provided them with camouflage for their illicit cargo.

Once the RPGs were loaded up, the crew spread the tarp over them and began to shovel a thin layer of gritty dirt on top. Peter left them to it. The physical labor had warmed him against the winter wind coming off the mountains, and he thought he caught a hint of sulphuric tang on the air. Probably from an old coal stove.

The men would bring up the cars shortly and he hoped Vera and Gina were ready to go and not off to see the inside of some church on the other side of town. He felt bad for telling Vera to stay put, but it hadn't been only the timing issue that had bothered him.

Vera and Gina might have become targets. Someone had broken into their room while he and Vera enjoyed a dinner out. He was mortally certain that they hadn't left the light on. Whoever got in was good – the starch Peter sprinkled by the door had been undisturbed. The intruder knew to avoid it. This told him it was someone who knew of his customary precautions. Someone he'd dealt with in the past. It had been someone without a key – as indicated by the scratch marks by the lock. Yet nothing was missing.

Two years ago, he would have explained all that to Vera and let her assess the risk for herself.

Having seen the crimson flower bloom on her tan coat back in Kiev had changed everything. Now he did all he could to shelter her from the rougher edges of his family's business dealings. It's not that she was unable to cope. She was brave and level-headed, and her marksmanship was decent for a novice. Peter didn't think he could deal with another Kiev, though. Two inches lower, and the results of their run-in with Uncle Ilya's rivals would have been very different.

He tripped over a cobblestone paver and righted himself, cursing at his lack of here-and-now. Peter had the grace of a panther under ordinary circumstances, but these were not it.

The expanded scope of his duties left him off kilter. He was impatient with the way the transaction had dragged out. He lacked humor for broken axels and lengthy forays into the countryside to rescue precious artifacts. All he wanted was to get to Vienna and deposit the considerable sum of money that now rested in his backpack.

Moreover, he found he lacked patience for Uncle Ilya and his battle with cancer. The thought had him awash in guilt as soon as it surfaced, yet he couldn't resent the inevitability with which the web of family ties and obligations had pulled him into a leadership position. That's exactly where he didn't want to be. His personal life had been jelling together just fine before all this nonsense.

He knew if he led the family, the move would awaken old jealousies and his cousins would resent him even more.

Oleg was in charge of the business end, Alexi was the security specialist. He preferred being called that, instead of just "muscle." It lent legitimacy to a profession where Alexi was no stranger to bruised knuckles, discharged rounds, and holding the local police over the barrel with a carefully assembled collection of compromising photographs.

Peter didn't want any of this. His stomach began to flip and the sidewalk shifted like sand under his feet. Sand, with the tide coming in. He glanced at his watch in what had become a nervous gesture. Then he let his mind drift toward Gina. Intelligent, fresh and unattached to all this, in her spunky ponytail, sporting an idealistic view of the world. Gina, who blushed when he held the door for her, or pulled out the dining chair. A small smile crept to his lips, and the butterflies in his stomach were suddenly diverted toward a target more attainable than being free of his family business obligations.

VERA WAS using the bathroom when the door opened and Peter walked in, bringing with him the brisk winter air. Gina looked up from her notebook. He looked like a man who'd let nothing stand in his path, and urgency rolled off him in waves.

"Where's Vera?" He barked.

Her first thought was, 'Did he know it was me?' and she felt as though her guilt was written on her forehead. She pushed the irrational fear aside as she recoiled at his tone of voice and straightened her spine to meet his gaze straight on

"In the bathroom. We're packed and ready to go."

"Go get her." Peter assessed their luggage. There was a sound of water running and then a door opened, and Vera emerged.

"No need. We've been ready for almost two hours." Gina heard a hint of a cutting edge in Vera's voice. It reminded her that this was, after all, Dr. Vera Christoff, a woman of substance who was not accustomed to being left waiting or ordered about.

"Sorry for being late. The cars are pulling up. Let's go." He grabbed a suitcase in each hand and wheeled them toward the door, giving the concierge a nod of acknowledgment. Gina thought there was no surprise in the older man's face at Peter's sudden lack of manners, and wondered whether Peter was a frequent guest here. If the smooth, suave and urbane Peter Christoff looked concerned, there was probably a reason for it.

Gina hurried out after him with her backpack over one shoulder and her duffle in the other hand. She smiled at the concierge. It was an 'I am sorry I can't be polite to you' smile, and he smiled back. Vera followed after. They tossed their luggage in the trunk of the heavy vehicles and settled in their seats.

"Don't speed," Peter told his driver. "We don't want to attract attention."

"They have what they want, no?" The driver said with a shrug. "No reason to give us trouble."

"That's why. They don't need us anymore."

CHAPTER 9

Gina curled into the padded leather of the car's back seat. Every pothole bounced the car up and down, which in turn bounced her and reminded her once again that she drank a lot of coffee that morning. The coffee, so necessary to wake her up, bothered her stomach unless she ate, and what she ate at the breakfast buffet was salty – requiring yet more coffee.

She looked out the window. They were on what passed for a large highway in the former Yugoslavia, a thin ribbon of concrete that wound through the arid mountains and connected tiny villages and remote towns. The cold draft off the car door made her shiver, which made her bladder feel even fuller. They just passed another village, yet the driver showed no desire to stop.

"What's wrong, Gina?" Vera asked from the seat next to her. "Are you ill?"

"Not exactly," Gina said, contorting her face with embarrassment.

"But… ?"

"I have to use the restroom." Gina felt like a little kid, saying that. She saw the older woman nod with understanding and turn toward the driver. "We need to stop, the sooner the better," she said, and Gina was pleased to understand every word.

"Impossible. We're under time pressure." The driver sounded tense.

"Peter," Vera turned to her husband, who sat in the front seat. "This is a bathroom emergency."

Peter turned to smirk at his wife, but then his eyes slid to Gina, and his face sobered with sudden understanding. "Ah," he said in English. "I'm

74

afraid there are no good places to stop along this road. We just passed several outposts, and there isn't much until we get closer to the border."

"But I really need to go." The words slipped out of her mouth all by themselves. Gina was beyond embarrassment.

"Okay. You'll need to go by the side of the road." Peter turned to the driver and gave him instructions in Russian.

"But… " Gina threw a beseeching look at Vera, who only shrugged.

"Don't worry about it. The guys and I have done this any number of times. The public toilet situation in most parts of Europe is very different from what you're used from the United States."

"I know. Usually, I get to plan ahead better." Gina focused on the scenery rushing by. They were careening down a hill, toward a bridge across a small river. Once they were almost to the other side, the driver signaled a right turn, and guided them down an old, abandoned forest lane. The river was to their right and a hill thick with pines was to the left. The road widened into a clearing. Several stacks of logs rimmed the perimeter, and the soft ground in the middle was rutted by heavy equipment. The driver turned around, and so did the two vehicles behind him.

"Vera, go with her," Peter said. His wife nodded. She pulled out her Glock and moved the slide back, chambering a round.

"Come on," she nodded at Gina. "You get to pee with a personal body guard."

Gina looked toward the river. Low shrubs grew there, affording a semblance of privacy. She stumbled as Vera yanked her shoulder in the other direction.

"Over there, behind the logs," she hissed. "The river's too open. You'd be seen from the road."

GINA SQUATTED behind the harvested lumber.

She felt intensely vulnerable. She had been vulnerable all along, but squatting to pee with the winter air freezing her parts with three cars of armed strangers only a few meters away drove it all home even harder. The wind was stingin her butt. There was nothing to dry with, and the pine

75

needles littering the ground were unlike the leaves she would've found while hiking the Appalachian Trail.

"Hurry!" Vera's voice was soft. Gina realized that all drivers turned their engines off. She stood up and fixed her jeans. Vera put her gun on a log beside her and relieved herself.

"Might as well," she said. The woods were silent, with only the wind rustling in the pines. When Vera was ready, gun in her hand, she peeked around the logs again. Just before she gave the go-ahead, Gina heard the roar of two engines coming down the same steep hill.

"Get down!" Vera hissed. They both flattened their bodies against the lumber. Gina smelled the sap only after she felt its stickiness on the sleeve of her jacket.

Her senses were heightened, as though she could taste the river on the winter breeze and hear every whisper of the wind. She met Vera's eyes, who shook her head. They listened to the cars roar past their little hideout and downshift up the next hill.

"Who was it?"

"I don't know," Vera said. "Count to thirty, then scurry to the car. Don't slam the door when you get in." She waited for Gina to nod. Then she took the gun in a two-handed grip and disappeared.

THIRTY SECONDS. More like forever. Gina strove not to increase her cadence of her counting. On thirty, she peeked around the logs. The three black sedans stood lined up, ready to exit. Gina ran from the logs to the last one in line in a crouch, then to the second one, then to her car in front.

She circled around its trunk, aware that it might be full of either weapons or stolen artwork. She slipped into the car and closed the door as gently as she could.

Five seconds later, Vera slid into the seat next to her. She closed her door with equal care and was about to empty the chamber of her weapon, when Peter stopped her action with a shake of his head.

"Not yet. It was them."

"Who?" Gina said.

76

Vera gave her a long look. "Peter sold some diamonds. This country has disintegrated – there's civil war now. You can't read the papers so you don't know, but Dubrovnik seems to be just the beginning of all this."

"Vera." Peter's voice held a note of warning.

"I'm not scaring her. She needs to know," Vera retorted. She turned to Gina again. "His customer wants the money as well as the goods. There's no police to enforce the law. The military's in charge, and the soldiers are easy to bribe."

Gina nodded. Thoughts swirled through her head, falling into place like chess pieces on a three-dimensional board. She saw avenues and possibilities. She saw Peter and Vera as part of an age-old system of wartime profiteers. Her data was biased by her sources.

Once again she regretted that she had not been able to read that official letter that allowed Peter Christoff to pass the Serbian checkpoint without a bribe, free and unmolested. Whoever issued that letter was part of the deal. The sudden insight only outlined her playing field, but it did not offer her a direction.

She had nothing to say, so she only nodded.

Peter Christoff was trading Stinger missiles for Soviet RPG's. She didn't know where the Stingers would end up, or who would use the RPG's. One thing was for certain - if Uncle Sam lost some of his toys, this wasn't a simple one-time heist. The leak must have been systemic and there was more where the first five Stingers came from.

Those missiles could very well end up hurting her cousin, just as stolen American armaments hurt her brother in Mogadishu. The dogs of war were loosed once again, and the fires of conflict now had their fuel. Gina pressed her back into the car seat and focused on keeping her breath steady.

She didn't know who she was with.

What part they were playing.

For whom.

Dr. Vera Christoff was more than just a soft-spoken, well-known art history scholar - she was also her husband's accomplice. Now that her lie tinted her character with an entirely different shade, Gina made a critical decision. She'd no longer protect Vera from Peter's infidelity. Gina was ready to do whatever it took to get her hands on that letter.

"WE HAVE to split. A convoy of three black sedans is too recognizable." Peter's knee was bouncing up and down at a steady rhythm. He hated sitting like this, trapped and passive. He could be patient – he had been patient in the past – but the money in his sack was like burning coal and he felt an urgent need to get it off his back and into a deposit box.

"We could switch cars." Vera's voice held a note of hesitation. She did not offer suggestions very often, because tactical decisions were his expertise. Except they weren't. Overall strategy and tactics was all Uncle Ilya, and after him, Oleg. Peter wished there was a telephone so that he could call California for a brief consultation. He still didn't know who broke into his room, or why they picked both the lock of the main door and breached the door from the balcony. Maybe they couldn't pick the lock and had to resort to the balcony route. Maybe two people broke in. The Bosnians as well as the Serbs.

He cut off the streams of speculations. They got him nowhere.

"We could disguise one of these cars, leave the second, and replace the third," he said after a few moments passed. Then he turned to his driver, and a discussion in Russian ensued. In the back of his mind, he was relieved to have a secret language handy. Gina sat in the back with her eyes almost closed. She could've been napping, and maybe she was. Then again, he didn't know her. The only thing going in Gina's favor right now was the way they met – an unexpected run-in at a location that had been Vera's last-minute lark.

Gina wasn't anyone's plant. He considered ditching her, but the thought was but a brief flutter in his mind. Art and travel, smooth skin and her shy smile, incredible naiveté. She almost made him smile.

Gina could stay and look pretty while he and his driver hammered out the last details of their strategy.

"YOU GIRLS GO mess up the third car," Peter said. "That one's loaded and has more gas."

"What are you looking for?" Vera asked. Gina watched their exchange with fascination. It seemed like Vera was no stranger to these kinds of operations. Who was Dr. Christoff, really?

"Just make it less shiny. Make it unworthy of being a part of this fleet."

"Okay. I need my luggage, then." Vera pulled out her toiletry bag. Gina watched her rummage and set a few things out. Then their eyes met."

"Come here, Gina. Have you ever aged a brand-new piece of sculpture before?"

"Only for Halloween."

"That's enough!" Vera smiled. "Now we'll age that car. I need you to take this hand cream and spread it all over the hood. Then we'll zap it with some powder. Let's see if this baby'll turn from shiny black to dull gray for us."

Gina warmed up the cream between her hands. The hood was still warm, and warm was good. It made the cosmetic go further, and it felt good besides. She saw Vera disappear in the underbrush of the riverbank with a shopping bag. "Where'd she go?" she asked Peter, alarmed.

"She'll be back, little bird, don't worry," he said, and as he looked at her, his face lit up with a warm smile that went all the way up to his eyes. "She'll just get some materials to make this car look less like the others."

"Why are we doing this, again?" She thought she knew, but was curious to see what he would say.

Peter looked up from behind the trunk. He had a screwdriver in one hand and a license plate in the other. "There's a good chance that the border guards are on a lookout for us. We want to look like someone else. Once we're in Hungary, we can clean all this off again." She watched him hide the old license plate under the floor rug in the rear passenger seat and pull out a new one. By the time he was done switching the plates, Gina turned the hood from shiny to sticky, and Vera returned from the river with a plastic Tesco shopping bag full of mud.

"I'll get started on the wheels," she said. "It would help if we could drive through a genuine puddle at high speed, but I'll see what I can do."

"COME, LET'S wash our hands," Vera told her only ten minutes later. The third car looked old and muddy, and held the few pieces of artwork from the second car. Two of Peter's men took the second car away, and Peter's driver plus the guards from the third car took long guns from a hidden compartment in the car's roof, checked the action, and faded into the trees that surrounded the clearing. Peter leaned his hip against the clean car, a small gun in his hand. He looked like a cat on a prowl, waiting, with his muscles going from tense to loose and back again. Gina had never seen a man with a weapon that tense before, and she would have stayed, had not Vera nudged her with her hip.

"I won't drag you this time, with my hands all muddy. Come on, you're a mess. Let's wash up." She led Gina down a steep bank. There were stones right by the river, and Gina was able to squat on a flat one and reach all the way down to the sparkling water surface. The river ran fast and clear and sounded cold. She put her hand in and almost yelped at the shock of it.

"Bracing, isn't it?" Vera said with a knowing smile in her voice. "Just do your best. We don't want to look like we don't belong in a clean car."

"I never expected this to turn in such cloak-and-dagger," Gina said as she shook the frigid water off her fingertips.

"Oh, it's not too bad," Vera said. "Really, considering the level of corruption in these little countries, especially during a state of war, we have been extremely lucky so far." There was no humor in her voice.

Gina shivered, and it wasn't just because of the river by her feet.

GINA MADE USE of the place behind the logs again, and took her time to stretch her stiff legs and back while she was under the cover of the tree line. The way people were acting, stretching out in the open might have attracted unwanted attention. Minutes clicked by. Peter and Vera disappeared behind the logs one at a time. Gina's stomach grumbled. She checked her watch, and was surprised to find it was well after noon already. When the wind picked up, she retreated back into the car. Vera was already there, reading some small-print journal with black-and-white photographs of old walls.

"I hope everything is okay," Gina said. "Is it normal for them to be gone this long?"

"No," Vera said, not lifting her eyes from the text. Before she could say more, an unfamiliar blue car rumbled into the clearing. "Ah, here they are. And look, they got a Skoda. That's good, there are lots of those in this part of the world."

The men emerged from the trees and hid their weapons in the two black sedans. The Skoda didn't have a good place for rifle storage and they had to cross the checkpoint with their armaments undetected.

"Let's go," Peter said. "We'll head straight for the border. If we get there around dinnertime, the guards will be less alert."

CHAPTER 10

The mountains turned to foothills. A river wound through the faraway lowlands like a fat and glistening snake. They made their way down – the blue Skoda first, their clean car second, and the third, dirty car bringing up the rear. Gina noticed the way the drivers spaced out along the winding road, no longer giving an appearance of an organized convoy. They weren't using their radios, either. Just a bunch of strangers, heading north.

"What's that river?" Gina whispered at Vera.

"Morava, I think. Not sure... there is a big town on it, Cacak. We'll fuel up and get something to eat. That should hold us until Hungary."

"That little river in the mountains, is that a tributary?" Gina wanted to orient herself in space as well as in time. She didn't even have a map and the uncertainty of her situation flipped her stomach with sudden vertigo. Her bags were right under her feet and she was wearing her jacket. She suppressed a sudden urge to grab her stuff, open the door, and bail out as the car slowed down in a curve of the road. She could hitchhike – there were no signs of war this far north, not yet. She sat still, thinking hard to what she remembered from the map, as well as from over two years of travel in the region.

Cacak was about two hour's drive through the mountains. away. Sixty miles – that would be a two-day's walk for a Roman legionnaire.

Gina suppressed a sigh and stayed put. She needed to hold on until they crossed the border, if not all the way to Vienna.

Gina leaned her forehead against the cold glass of the window. She was looking down a huge hill, debating her options, when the car swerved a sharp right. She sat up and braced herself, but the driver got them from the brink of a ditch.

"Fucking idiot," Peter said as the delivery van careened past them. "He almost ran us off the road!"

"A coincidence?" Vera asked.

"Probably." Peter asked the driver to slow down, and sure enough, the dirty car appeared behind them within a minute. "Good. They seem to be okay."

The driver floored it, taking turns down the mountain with alarming speed. The dirty car followed at a safe distance, but within line of sight. The troops decided to stick together, Gina thought, and she grasped the handle above her seat in anticipation of a wild ride.

They almost passed the blue Skoda. Had it not been for the grove of young saplings down the hill, they would have never seen its powder-blue color against the evergreen boughs. The car was down a precipice, driven off a cliff. There was no smoke, no fire. Just a small sedan, stuck in the trees down a steep hill like a child's toy.

Both cars pulled over. Gina made to get out with the others, but Peter stopped her with a stern look. "Stay here. We don't know what happened."

She stayed while Peter and the bodyguard from the other car rigged a rope down the cliff, and disappeared. She looked at Vera in search of information. The older woman sat still, her Glock in her hand. She turned left, then right.

"What's going on?" Gina hated the way her voice shook, and the way she couldn't contain her curiosity.

"That van must have run them off the road. When he took a run at us, we were on an inside curve. We got lucky."

Gina rolled down the window. The smell of broken pines mingled with the heady reek of spilled gasoline. A raptor cried overhead. "I wish we could see."

"I have a job for you," Vera said. "I want you to turn around in your seat and keep an eye on the road behind us. I'll look ahead of us. It could be they aren't working alone."

"Who are they?" Now that she had a job, the tremble was gone from her voice.

"Greedy customers, probably," Vera said. She didn't turn toward Gina to meet her eyes, scanning the road ahead of them instead, and the hill to the left. Gina followed her example and fixed her eyes on the terrain to their rear.

"I wish I had a gun," she blurted out. There was a beat of silence before Vera allowed a hint of smile into her tone of voice.

"But how would you know who to shoot?"

PETER DUG his toes into the crumbling rock under the overhang and grasped the rope nice and tight. He looked up. It wasn't too bad. No worse than the gym. Not being belayed gave him a moment's hesitation, but then he thought of the awesome feeling of exhilaration he always had when he made it up the wall, and he forced a smile.

Just like in the gym.

He kicked out to swing away from the rock a bit, lifted his feet, and anchored them on the protruding, jagged shale. He didn't trust the rock to free-climb it. The face was weathered and friable, and even though free-climbing was easier on a solid rock, Peter would never attempt it on an unstable surface.

He grabbed at the rope hand over hand a few times and pulled himself up as his feet did the walking. Two meters and five minutes later – because dragging it out would just make him tired for no reason – he was at the edge of the cliff, hanging onto the rope and trying to swing his leg up and over.

The weight he put on the rope forced it flush against the rock, but the top had a bit of soil on it and some dead weeds, and Peter dug his bare hands into the soil and under the woven skein that kept him from crashing on top of the blue Skoda sedan. Dirt and broken plant fragments made their way up his nose and he almost sneezed. The grit of soil in his mouth was a welcome distraction from the stench of gasoline. He tried not to think about it, and crawled over the top of the precipice on his hands and knees. He ignored the tear of fabric that split the air and he pushed away the chill that drifted up his thigh. When he was a little boy, Aunt Yelena used to yell at him for climbing in his good clothes. When she heard about this little snag in their business trip, she would be happy that he did.

He stumbled toward the clean car and opened the passenger door. Vera sat on guard, a gun in her hand, scanning the road and hillside ahead of them. Their tagalong, Gina, kept an eye on their rear.

Vera slid a glance in his direction, not taking her grey eyes off the road. "Well?"

"The car's gonna blow. We moved the guys out, but they're hurt. They're moving the goods out of the trunk right now. I'll tell the others to pull the stuff up. The climb up is a bitch."

"Is there a way around?" Vera asked, and he could only marvel at her calm.

"Nothing easier than this, and the only way to anchor the rope is against a car. This is as good as it gets."

Now Vera looked him up and down, taking in the bleeding cuts on his filthy hands, the dirt in his face, and his torn clothes. "You're a mess."

"Yeah. That's fixable."

"Anything us girls can do to help?"

"Just what you're doing." He leaned over to peck a kiss on her cheek. The gesture surprised him. He didn't expect to feel the need to do that, but the old guilt welled up.

The scar, the blood.

Vera's urge to leave all this behind.

He failed her once again. After she got shot in Kiev, he swore she'd never have to watch his back with a gun in her hand again, yet here she was. Dr. Avery "Vera" Christoff, his wife and accomplice in things she hated and did not understand.

"Thank you," he said. Then he closed the door and walked off to the dirty car and talked with the two armed men who frowned at him from the front seats.

"WE'RE STILL too recognizable," Vera said. She said it in English for Gina's benefit. "We'll need to get gas and food, and they will be watching for us."

"We better lose some people," Peter said as he surveyed their group of eight. Six men, two women, all travelling together. "We're conspicuous."

"You can drop me off outside of town," Gina said in a small voice. She had contemplated splitting off only half an hour ago, but now that there was a tangible enemy on their heels, the strength of the pack – any pack – provided at least some protection.

"Nonsense," Vera said. "Peter, we can hide her in the back, and we can hide the guys, too. These cars are roomy enough, it shouldn't be an issue."

The spilled gasoline odor still trailed them from the clothing of the men.

"You need to change," Vera said. "I can drive the other car."

"You won't be driving," one of the driver's replied in Russian, but Peter cut him off.

"No, that's a good idea. They won't be looking for a woman driver."

"If we had disguises, would that work?" Gina said. They did already disguise a car.

"They know what we're driving," Peter groaned. "They must have followed the blue Skoda."

"And they know the clean car, but nobody took a run at the dirty car," Vera said. "That's where the goods are right now, too. I'll drive the dirty car, and Gina can hide in the back with one of the guys. We'll change clothes as much as possible. I'll wear makeup. But quickly!"

"I FEEL LIKE the Three Stooges," Peter grumbled, which wasn't something Gina saw him do often. Despite his attitude, he let Vera age his eyes with a smudge of dark eyeliner and judicious powder application. He was already dressed in a clean business uniform. The bodyguard from the dirty car and the injured driver from the blue Skoda – Sergei? - sprawled in the back, and Gina realized with dismay that she was learning their names only now, after days on the road.

They might've been fake names – hard to tell. In any case, Peter's men didn't waste words. The two in the back of his car had a blanket and a few light pieces of luggage waiting until they got closer to Cacak.

86

"Peter will hide you when it's time," Vera told them. Then she turned to Peter. "Ready?"

"Always," he said. "Although, I must say, you don't look bad at all with all that war paint on your face." He laughed when she gave him a baleful glare from underneath her long, artificially black eyelashes. The carmine lipstick matched the red sweater she so rarely wore. "Although you won't fool anyone with that hostile attitude!"

"I should've added a black wart onto your nose," she said with her own nose lifted up high. She nodded to Gina. "Let's get going!"

GINA AND the injured driver, whose name was Zhenia, sat in the back, and the original driver of the dirty car, Anton, sat in the passenger seat. He twitched every time Vera shifted gears or entered a turn at a speed that was a bit too fast, or a bit too slow. She knew he had a gun under his green windbreaker.

They were out of disguise aids, and they were in a hurry, so Peter sacrificed his long, woolen coat to act as their hiding blanket. As it sat over Gina's knees now, she smelled just a hint of sandalwood rise up to her nose.

She smiled. Peter always smelled just like the faintest bit of wood and warmth. It wasn't an overpowering scent, nothing like a sandalwood incense. She didn't care for incense, but whatever wafted out of Peter and his coat made her feel warm and cared for.

For now, Gina strategized on how to best share space with the man next to her. He'd been hurt, his shoulder was probably dislocated. It could have been a broken bone. They had no way of finding out, not yet. She might have minded snuggling up with the Russian-speaking stranger to her right, but she didn't mind hiding under the generous warmth of Peter's coat. As she relished the last calories of his body heat that made their way from his coat to her thighs, she thought to the warmth of his smile and the enticing kiss they had shared.

Peter was candy. But Vera was in the driver's seat in front of her, a woman whose ratings oscillated between the ones of Gina's idol, and Peter's accomplice. Every time Gina thought the shine had worn off the famous art personage, she found something new to admire. There was a steady quality to Vera Christoff in which she held a gun, or diverted Gina's

87

fretting into guard duty, or compelled the men to remain still while she applied makeup to their faces. She was like a den mother supervising a Scout expedition gone wrong. When events resembled normalcy, Peter was in charge in every way. Yet once the shit hit the fan, it was his wife who formulated a strategy and compelled them to carry it out. Gina didn't know whether to admire her or be even more suspicious of her.

As Gina hid her hands under Peter's coat in order to soak up the guilty pleasure of his presence, she felt a hard edge of creased paper. The coat had a breast pocket, and the piece of paper jutted out of it.

She had felt that texture in her hands before, right before she failed to photograph it. The mysterious letter, written in Serbian and marked by an official-looking letterhead and seal, was at the edge of her fingertips.

CHAPTER 11

"Okay, you back there. Get down." Vera said it in both English and Russian, and Gina folded her body onto the seat obediently. She felt Vera – or Anton – reach all the way back and pull her coat over her head.

She drew in a deep breath as she rested her head on her backpack. Her legs stretched off the seat and into the neighboring space, jostling the knees of her injured neighbor. She felt him wedge his body behind hers, all stiff and awkward. They were strangers, forced into a position that could have been intimate otherwise.

Gina stiffened at the unwanted contact. A whole guy was plastered to her back, her butt, her legs. She felt his breath against her back, trapped under Peter's coat. Somebody dropped smaller luggage on top of them, and Gina felt the injured guy drop a curse she didn't understand as something heavy landed on his bad shoulder.

Knowing that the man behind her was in pain made the indignity of her position tolerable. She would not add to it on account of preserving her maidenly virtue, or whatever they used to call that thing in the olden days. They were just two people stuck together in the backseat of a large, black sedan, going through town. The locals probably considered the city of Cacak a metropolis, with its population well over hundred thousand souls, and it probably was, compared to the small mountain villages to the south. It was bound to have more than one hospital. Gina wished they could have stopped and dropped off the injured, but the verdict was to soldier through to Hungary first.

THE CENTRIPETAL force pushed her head into the door. Moments later she slid the other way and crushed her fellow stowaway. The first time she inadvertently slid into him, he moaned in pain. The second time, she made sure to hold onto the edge of the seat under her. Time passed in uncounted impressions of sound and movement, and the scent of Peter's coat over her head became overbearing.

"Hold on back there. We're entering town. We'll stop for gas and food, and we'll share out the food once we get through." Vera's voice was muffled under the layers that concealed Gina and Zhenia.

"Get some Advil or something. He's in pain." The sharp tone of her own voice surprised her. Vera didn't respond to her, but mumbled a question in Russian.

"Eto nichevo." *It's nothing.* If the death grip on Gina's calf was any indication, the man was understating his condition a good bit. It occurred to her that she never bothered to learn his name.

"Molodiec." *Good man.* Anton's word of praise caused the hand on Gina's calf loosen somewhat.

They must have known. Both Vera and Anton knew of the pain, and the extent of the injury, yet he didn't seek out any help. Either they were possessed of extraordinary greed, or their situation was a lot more serious than they let on. Either way, Gina felt the small spark of anger grow bright and hot.

He should have gotten those two some help. Any help. They had passed through smaller villages, but even those had a pharmacy, or a nurse, or someone. Something.

The rumble of wheels on a rough pavement reverberated through her body, and the grip on her calf tightened again.

Cobblestones.

She pressed her butt into his chest. It wasn't much as hugs went, but it was the best she could do at the time. That's when she realized that they both relaxed, resigned to their predicament. Modesty took second seat to surviving undetected.

The rough vibrations turned to a smooth hiss of modern pavement.

"We'll take gas now," Vera said in her bilingual way. Gina was almost tempted to let her know that Russian was just fine when a shift of a bag above her pressed a corner of scratchy something into her cheek.

90

The letter.

The letter was still in Peter's coat pocket. It was there because Gina, who had no compunction about photographing it, had reservations against stealing it.

Stealing was not okay.

It was something she'd have to fess up to later, and besides, suppose they needed it at the border again?

A door opened and closed, and the car wobbled as the driver stepped out to get gas.

"Can you see the others?" Gina said, but there was no answer. She didn't know whether Peter didn't want to look like he was a madman talking to himself, or whether it was Peter who left the vehicle to do the errands.

The letter scratched her cheek some more. She thought back to the missiles. Official sales didn't happen just like that, in sheltered parking lots of small spa towns in the mountains.

Unofficial sales were bad news.

She pried her fingers off the vinyl seat beneath her and slid her hand up her face, nice and slow. She grasped the paper and teased it out of the breast pocket of Peter's coat. Its rustle was like the crack of a breaking branch in the forest to her ears and she paused, waiting.

No reaction. Her traveling companion did not react, nor did she hear any sounds from the front of the car. Gina manipulated the folded paper under her body as though it had slipped out by accident, and she happened to be lying on it.

She'd wait till the border – just in case.

Maybe Peter wouldn't miss it right away. There was nothing else in that pocket, and she could only presume that he had his wallet and all other necessary things elsewhere. If the letter was needed to cross the border, then she would find it on the floor and hand it over. It was a compromise, and the thought of relinquishing the document filled her with misgivings. It was important. She just didn't know why.

VERA WAITED across the street. She glanced at her watch as though she was expecting someone and they were late, but her eyes never left the clean, black sedan at the gas station on the corner. The driver was checking the tires and Peter was in the little store inside. There were no self-serve pumps like in some parts of the US, which meant an attendant would see them all. That's why she didn't pull in and take care of her fuel and food at the same time. It felt like forever before Peter emerged with a few bottles of fizzy lemonade and a few road snacks. There was no real food, drive-through fast food was unheard of in these parts, and they couldn't risk a restaurant. They had passed a grocery store, but Peter's car did not pull in.

Vera knew the location was too exposed, and the process of wading through an unfamiliar layout would have taken too much time. They would just make do.

Peter and his driver got back into their car. There had been no sign of movement in the back seat of Vera's car while she was gone. Gina was holding it together, then. That was good to know. She'd been concerned for the other man and his ability to travel injured. Her wounded charge had a concussion and a number of bruises, and maybe a broken clavicle. Vera recognized the pinched look on Zhenia's face, and the care with which he inserted his tall frame into the backseat of the car. She regretted that they didn't even make him a sling out of a spare T-shirt, but there had been no time back then. Maybe later, once they made their way out of town.

She watched Peter disappear and started counting. When she reached two hundred, she started the car and eased it into traffic. She drove around the block and approached the gas station from the opposite direction, ordered fuel, and pulled out her wallet. The price of gas must have tripled since the Serbs sailed forth against Dubrovnik, and the attendant demanded Deutschmarks instead of the local currency. They knew this might happen, but were low on Deutschmarks and decided to keep them for later. With a charming, Italian smile she offered to pay in Italian liras. She tossed in a phrase or two, relying on the everyday courtesies that she knew she could say with a Roman accent. The attendant's face beamed at the sight of hard currency and filled her tank.

"Grazie. Buon journo!" He probably overcharged her.

"Ciao!" she beamed at him, engaged the engine, and took off. Peter had a head start. She wended her way over the cobblestones and back onto the artery that pulsed through town, carrying people in and out. She crossed the Morava river and continued heading north. They were out of the mountains now and into the fertile plains, a land that was well defended over the centuries. She was right outside of city limits when she passed a shiny, black sedan pulled over by the side of the road.

Peter.

He saw her. Few cars later, he peeled into the traffic again and follow her to the Serbian region of Vojvodina. The road was smooth and new, and the fresh asphalt hummed under her wheels.

"Is everyone doing fine back there?" she asked.

"Great. Just like sardines," Gina replied. "But I'm

"Shut up," Zhenia ground out. "Loudmouth."

Gina understood the common cuss words perfectly, and thought that he would have used the equivalent of "fucking loudmouth." Since he did not, Gina surmised his headache was almost unbearable.

"We will stop soon," Vera said in a soothing tone, speaking Russian.. "There is a place an hour north of here that is sheltered. You'll be fine."

"GINA. GINA! You can sit up now." Peter Christoff's voice came as though from afar, and Gina realized she had fallen asleep. There was no sense of movement or sound. She felt someone – presumably Peter – remove the smaller pieces of luggage that weighed down his coat and helped conceal them in the back seat. She wiggled up slowly, careful not to jostle the man behind her. From the look of his eyes, he looked like he drifted off to sleep as well.

"Is everything okay? Where are we?" Gina's questions conveyed a sense of unease as she realized the front seats were empty. She looked out the windows and shivered – and that's when she noticed the small droplets on the car's windows. "It's raining again?"

"Snowing," Peter said. "It's not sticking yet, but it will. The weather's turning lousy, which is to our advantage."

She wondered why, but didn't asked, because a dark figure approached the driver's door and opened it, letting the chill air inside the car. Vera slid into the driver's seat, and Peter closed Zhenia's door and made himself uncomfortable riding shotgun.

The car was a cocoon of private warmth in the darkness, and Vera didn't disturb the peace by starting the engine just yet. "How are they?" she asked. "Zhenia, kak dela?" She was asking the man how he was doing.

"Khorosho," he whispered, obviously lying through his tobacco-stained teeth. His face was pale and he was unable to suppress the fine tremors that were running through his body. Vera nodded, then turned to Gina. "Get out. We're using the bathroom, like before. And hurry up."

Gina poured out her side of the car. The wind bit right through her hoodie and she wished she had the jacket that was somewhere on the bottom of car. The sooner she got her muh-needed business done, the faster she'd be back in the cozy compartment.

"Zhenia is in real pain," she said in Vera's direction as they jumped the ditch and entered a copse of bare trees. The land was flat around them. She felt like she could see far if she stood on a roof of a car.

"I know. Everybody knows. I got some medicine for him, but it won't help much. We'll stabilize his arm and move on. He'll go to a hospital as soon as we cross the border."

"Why can't he go here?" Gina asked.

"We can't stay with him and risk that whoever took a run at us will find us and do it again. We can't leave him behind, at their mercy. We're not leaving you behind either, even though you offered. They don't know you're not part of this, and you don't need to have them questioning you." There was a hard edge to Vera's voice as she pushed her way through the thin branches. One of them whipped at Gina and stung her cheek.

"Sorry," Vera said. "This is as much privacy as we get out here."

"What am I pissing at?" she asked as she squatted into the biting wind.

"When you get home, you can say you claimed Vojvodina in a traditional manner."

"Only if I was a guy," Gina said with a snort. "Guys care about stuff like that."

"So do we," Vera said. "Except our plumbing provides an extra challenge. I swear, this is just so unfair. None of the guys have to hang his butt out into the sleet like we do!"

THE ENVELOPE WAS secure under Gina thigh when they settled in the car again, eating local candy bars and drinking fizzy lemonade. It would have to hold them until Hungary.

She looked out the window. The sleet was driving against the pane. There used to be people who lived here and had endured this kind of weather in the open, riding their horses or mules or just walking home from the fields. Her imagination summoned a Roman legion on the march once again, all red and bronze and muscle.

She felt spoiled then. Soft. It helped her forget about the niceties of indoor plumbing.

Zhenia took two pills and chased them down with sticky lemonade. He made a face. She smiled at him, and he met her eyes and forced a smile back. She couldn't talk to him without betraying her knowledge of Russian, yet she wanted to lend him at least some support.

He was unshaven, but his hair was short and dark. Pain lines were etched into his face, making him seem older than he was. Gina guessed him to be around thirty. He didn't eat a thing yet.

She pointed to a candy bar and quirked her eyebrows. He shrugged, but the gesture made him spit an unfamiliar curse. Anton up front chuckled under his breath and said something to Vera, who glanced at Gina through the rearview mirror with curiosity. "What's wrong?"

"He's not eating," she said. "Does he want me to unwrap the food for him?"

Vera raised her eyebrows as Zhenia's predicament became clear, and fired off a question in his direction.

"Da."

"He says yes," Peter nodded to Gina. "Good thinking."

Which is how Gina ended up unwrapping the cheap chocolate and hazelnut bar for her neighbor. He was able to use his left hand and picked it up, nodding at her in thanks. She smiled back, then turned away to give him privacy.

She tried not to think about Zhenia and his brave front, or that he was pretty darn cute. Maybe he wasn't as devastatingly handsome as Peter Christoff, but Peter Christoff was an immovable, indestructible rock of the group. Zhenia used to look intimidating in that generic body-guard way, which was why Gina tuned him out before. Now she saw a man barely half a decade older than she was, and just as lost. Peter Christoff was an arms dealer of dubious repute, but this guy next to her, he seemed somehow more human and more approachable in his broken imperfection. She chanced him another glance. The half-eaten chocolate was in his left hand. His right arm hung useless in a sling, and his eyes darted between the chocolate bar and his half-finished bottle of lemonade, as though he knew what he wanted, but wasn't sure what steps to take to get to it.

Very slowly, Gina reached for the bottle the man was holding between his knees. She unscrewed its metal cap and removed his candy bar from his left hand. He took the bottle from her by himself and drank. He didn't meet her eyes, and Gina noted how a flush of red crept up his neck and up to his cheeks.

She strove to maintain a neutral expression. No smiles, no flirty glances. There was no use making him feel any more useless than he was already feeling.

Men. Why is accepting help so damn hard for them?

Her feminist self railed against the other sex in her mind. Zhenia was, no doubt, a product of traditional upbringing somewhere in the boondocks of Mother Russia, and he didn't yet know that accepting help while injured was not a sign of weakness.

He finished his drink. She capped it and offered the chocolate back. He shook his head, smiled a hesitant and silent thank-you, and faced straight ahead.

Vera coughed to clear her throat, but her amusement was unmistakable. "If you lovebirds are all ready back there, we'll be on the way. Gina, make sure he doesn't spill his drink."

"Okay," she said, and tightened the cap on the glass bottle.

"We'll be at the border by dark. Before we approach, you two will need to hide again."

CHAPTER 12

"It's time to get down, you two. We are two hours away from the border." Vera's voice was an irritated command from the front of the dark vehicle.

"I have a passport," Gina said. "I'll be okay."

Few beats of silence passed. "We have passports that will suit. You saw Peter change the license plates."

Anton shuffled an envelope of paperwork in the passenger seat, and rifled through a small stack of documents until he picked out several official-looking pieces of paper and passport booklets. Then he ripped open the dry-zip edge of the car's ceiling lining and shoved the manila envelope with the remaining documents into a secret compartment. Gina only caught a dark outline of the weapons before he smoothed the ceiling material again.

"Presently, my name is Christie Peters, and I am British," she said with the faintest hint of a British accent that reminded Gina of old Monty Python movies. "Anton here is James and he can do the same thing, but your buddy in the back doesn't have an alternate ID, and we don't want him to trip any hotwires. And if he has to hide, you have to hide, too." She turned and gave Gina a beseeching look. "I am really, really sorry about the inconvenience. You are being a real trooper, but I need you to do it again." Vera looked her over and gave her a conspiratorial wink. "I wish it was me, hiding out in the back seat with him. Just tough it out for now. Few weeks from now, all this will look like a great adventure."

Gina felt her cheeks flush. She would've never guessed Vera for a saucy broad, saying such a thing in front of the others. Her thoughts of Peter's warm sandalwood scent and the novelty of his courtly manner gave way to embarrassed vertigo at the hands of his wife.

She wanted to grab her hair, and yank hard.

"Okay," she said instead, arranged her backpack, and looked at Zhenia. He sat upright next to her with his arm was in a sling, favoring his clavicle. "And as soon as we cross the border, we get him to a hospital, right?"

The man next to her twitched the slightest bit and as his eyes widened in surprise, Gina realized that she wasn't the only one with secret language skills.

Well, well, well.

She settled down, leaving as much space as she could manage. Soon, she felt Zhenia's heavy warmth envelop her from behind and heard a grunt of pain as he folded himself into the compressed space. Then there was the coat and the darkness and the cloying and presently unwelcome smell of Peter's coat, and the smooth rumble of the asphalt road. Gina expected Zhenia to reach out and grip her calf again, just to feel stable, but he didn't and she remembered that his whole arm, hand and all, were now tucked into his improvised sling.

She missed the casual contact in the dark. The darkness brought forth anxious thoughts she could not share. Such as, why did Peter Christoff not know that one of his bodyguards spoke English well enough to follow their conversation?

She wished she had paid more attention to the men that surrounded the Christoffs, and as she stayed curled in the warm darkness, she tried to recall every single detail about them. How well did Peter know them, really? They must have been local hires, and she grew curious as to their references and connections. Her sympathy for Zhenia's injury did not eliminate that certain and pervasive sense of suspicion that followed her ever since she was offered a ride out of Podgorica.

VERA TURNED on her windshield wipers again and slowed down some more. When two cars passed her, she resumed her speed, keeping the clean car of their diminished caravan far ahead of her.

"You okay back there?" she asked the two concealed people, and smiled when her only reply was a grunt and a curse.

"As soon as we get to Horgos, we'll swing by a hospital," she said.

Another muffled curse made its way out of the pile of blankets and luggage in the back seat. She couldn't resist and poke the bear some more. "You're lucky it was the Skoda that got ran off the road, Zhenia. If you two had to share the backseat of a car that small, I think one of you would have to travel strapped to the roof rack!"

"Look, you're the boss's wife but that doesn't mean you have to be such a bitch." The Russian words flowed in a melodious rhythm that belied their meaning. She smiled. You could say almost anything in Russian and make it feel nice and polite to the American ear.

"We'll be there in fifteen. You need another ibuprofen?"

Her offer fell on deaf ears, and she focused on the traffic around her. The Horgos border crossing was large, with six booths in each direction. This was an advantage, because she could hang back and see which customs agent processed Peter's car. She planned to use a different one, making sure that they passed several cars apart. It was all planned ahead and prearranged. Their alternate passports were on the ready.

She felt her hands tighten on the wheel and her shoulders stiffen, and forced several long, slow breaths before she could relax again.

THE BORDER crossing was chaos. There were lines of cars, bicycles, and pedestrians trying to make their way out of Serbia. The traffic coming in from Hungary was virtually nil. The queues of cars inched forward in the driving sleet. She saw the pedestrians huddle in family groups by the building in the middle, waiting their turn. With the dogs of war loose in the Balkans, surrounding countries were facing hordes of refugees.

It occurred to her that the hospital in Horgos might be full. She bit back the thought and focused on getting through the border undetected.

Vera wondered whom Peter pissed off this time, and how. She knew what would happen once they made it to safety, too. They would hunker down in a nice hotel somewhere out of the way, and her husband's roving eye would turn to Gina again. The young and innocent Gina, who was her competent assistant and whom she wanted for a friend.

If Peter did his zipper-malfunction thing, thought, she could kiss that idea good-bye. The fact that they had an arrangement didn't mean she had to cozy up to every bit of fresh flesh he dragged in off the street.

The cars moved ahead a few lengths. By the time they were next in line, their hood was covered with an inch of snow.

"It's lucky we got out of the mountains before the snow came," the bodyguard said.

"Very lucky," Vera agreed. "And even better, all the cars look alike right now, and the night is falling. As long as our documents hold up, we'll be fine."

THE OFFICIAL stamped the passport that belonged to Christie Peters and said, "Have a nice day" with the sort of an accent that showed it was one of very few phrases he knew.

"Thank you," Vera said with a nod. She did not smile. People did not smile at border crossings. The customs agents liked to feel their power, and smiling usually meant you had something to hide. An expression of neutral dignity was the best way to go.

And they were waved through. It was almost anticlimactic. She drove on to clear the area as she looked for a good place to pull over and wait for Peter's car. All the cars looked alike now, covered with wet snow, with lights on, and she was relieved to blend in so naturally.

"Welcome to Hungary," she said. "Now I need to find somewhere to park. Gina, you can sit up now." Then she repeated the same thing in Russian for Zhenia's benefit. The town of Horgos was not too far ahead. She didn't see Peter anywhere behind him, and he could not recognize any of the cars that passed them by.

"Get the radio," she nudged Anton. "Let them know we'll be at the hospital."

"Not safe yet. He could be stuck back there." The man said with a frown. "I'll give them ten minutes."

"Ten minutes," Vera agreed. Then she started the engine again, and made his way down the narrow, tree-lined streets of Horgos in search of first aid for their wounded companion.

THE HOSPITAL was one of those concrete, Communist-era complexes that had virtually no parking, because it was assumed that if the sick and injured were well enough not to need an ambulance, they were also well enough to use public transportation.

Vera's passengers were now all sitting upright.

"They better be in there somewhere," the bodyguard grumbled. "We should have never gotten separated."

"Call them on the radio," Vera said again, and the driver pulled a walkie-talkie from under the seat and turned it on. The crackle of static seemed to take forever before somebody replied on the other end.

"Hello?" Peter's voice was cautious. "The place is swamped. The best they can do is first aid. Park by the front entrance, the guard knows to expect you."

Vera was in gear and moving before he even finished. "Anton, help Zhenia out. Zhenia, you'll go by yourself. Peter's inside. Go on, you clowns. I'll stay with the car. Peter's probably using the rest of his family's bribe money just to get you seen by a real doctor."

She watched him walk off slowly. Only the original driver of this vehicle stayed. She saw Anton feel the small of his back.

"You didn't cross the border armed, did you?"

He gave her an incredulous look. "Yeah," he finally said. "So?"

"We could've been searched. Peter said everyone's weapons were to be cached."

"Peter also said he'd castrate me if anything happened to you."

"So did he travel armed, too? Suppose we got stopped. Hungary has been pretty easy-going with foreigners, but still. Don't you think you took an unreasonable risk?" As she spoke, Vera felt cold fury grip her gut and not let go. Stupid macho posturing. All of them, Peter included, have fallen victim to too many Hollywood movies.

"If those guys were gonna take a run at us, they'd have done it right before the border crossing, figuring we put the guns away." The driver got a stubborn set to his chin in the dark, briefly illuminated by the light of his cigarette. "You're pretty fucking naïve for a mob wife. Did you know that?"

Her spine straightened as she gripped the steering wheel. "I am not a mob wife. I am an art professor. And if you know what's good for you, you'll restrain your language in my presence."

"Huh." He drew on his cig again.

"And don't smoke in the car."

He turned his head toward her just as she turned toward him. He leaned in, big and looming. "You ain't the boss of me."

She didn't flinch, and she didn't back down. "Peter will be interested in this conversation."

He shrugged, crossed his legs, and put his cigarette out against the sole of his shoe. "It ain't my job to be nice'n'polite around the ladies. My job's to keep 'em alive."

HOURS FELT like days, and Vera's butt hurt from sitting for so long. She would have liked knowing what the situation was, but Peter knew where they were, and he'd send for them if anything came up. She got out of the car and paced back and forth on the concrete sidewalk just to feel her blood moving again, and then she did a few rudimentary stretches that made her feel good while she was doing them, but which were never an adequate solution to many hours on the road.

The wind picked up, bringing more sleet. Vera ducked back inside the car. The driver extinguished his cigarette on the sole of his boot again, sulking in his silence. Vera turned the key in the ignition to get more heat in the car.

Three hours.

Waiting wasn't bad in itself, but if Peter let her know what to expect, she could have secured rooms for all of them, and she could have been waiting somewhere warmer. Vera was just about to ask the driver to radio Peter again when somebody rapped on her car window. She jumped and turned and there was Peter, with the collar of his coat turned up against the weather.

She rolled the window down. "Hey."

"Hey. So, they're being seen right now. I left enough cash with them to see them through, but we need to move on. There are no more rooms anywhere in this town, with all the refugees. I want you to look at the map and decide where to go next. We need to sleep somewhere inside. Somewhere reasonably secure."

"Can't believe you're leaving them in the hospital," the driver said, as a gust of wind carried prickles of ice inside the car.

"No choice," Peter said levelly, although Vera noticed the way the lines around his eyes tightened. "You two find a place. I'll go and make the staff feel appreciated."

TO ANTONT'S great displeasure, Vera drove around the small town for quite a while in search of a pub. She didn't care. They have all earned a solid meal, and there was no telling where they would end up five hours from now.

She peered through the wet streaks left by the windshield wipers in an effort to make out the Hungarian street signs. The stores were all probably closed at five or six, and the only establishments with lights on served food and drink. This made her task a lot easier. She settled on a pub on the north end of Horgos, right by the main road out. She made sure they'd be open for at least two more hours before she headed back to the hospital.

Peter was already waiting for them. "I was getting worried, and nobody answered the radio."

"We were probably out of range," she said. "There's a place where we can eat. According to the map, our best bet for finding a hotel is Szeged, about an hour drive north of here, as long as the roads don't get slick."

"Good work. Get out of the car," Peter said.

104

"What?"

"Please get out of the car, dear."

Still feeling a bit off-center, Vera climbed out and faced him. "Yes? What's next? Do we still have enough money in cash? How much did you spend at the hospital?"

"Shh. We're fine. I just wanted to say, well done." He pulled her close and buried his face in her hair, never mind the sleet and the audience.

"Tough day today, but we're here, alive and kicking, okay? Zhenia is being seen and has pain pills. His driver only has a concussion. We still have cash. So relax."

She gave herself a moment to sump against Peter's chest, plastering herself to him in an effort to extract some heat through his sodden woolen coat. This felt like the old days, when everything was alright and Peter still hung the moon. The days when they were a team and his recreational sex didn't get between them.

The days before Kiev. Before she walked into a bullet. Before she got that star-shaped scar where her trapezius used to be.

As though he read her thoughts, Peter rubbed the healed wound with his gloved hand and kissed her temple. The moment passed. They split and hit the road again.

CHAPTER 13

BY THE TIME they made it to Szeged, the hot meal in Horgos was but a distant memory. Gina kept her eyes open through force alone, fueled by the need to know where they were.

Szeged was a bigger town than Horgos. The locals probably called it a city. Its wide streets were lined with trees, and the sidewalks were lit by wrought-iron street lamps. She noted the rococo flavor of the masonry ornamentation. The main drag definitely had an imperial flavor to it. It was quite possible some noble taxed his peasants to death just to make Szeged look a bit more like Vienna.

This hotel must have been the seventh they tried. When they did actually have a vacancy, it came as a surprise. Such a nice place, and it wasn't even full?

Gina peered out the window, inspecting architecture that hinted at centuries of imperial opulence. They had passed a museum along the way, which meant this would be one of the better places in town. Hotel Tisza-Szeged was probably too expensive had she visited here on her own. Regardless where Peter's money came from, his generosity extended even to luxury accommodations, and Gina found it in her heart to be genuinely grateful.

They parked.

As Gina stirred to help Zhenia unbuckle his seatbelt in the dark, the smooth paper of Peter's official letter of passage slipped under her jeans.

She glanced around.

Vera was gathering a few items up front, ready to step out of the car. The men were out of sight, and Zhenia managed the door handle by the dim dome light without her help.

Slick and smooth, she folded the letter and slipped it into her pants. That would have to do for now – and she'd hide it in her backpack once she made her way into the privacy of the bathroom.

The theft left her flushed, and she was relieved at the fresh kiss of wintry air that met her outside.

Minutes later, they were hauling small bits of luggage through a lobby that gleamed with carved, polished wood and gilded frames on the walls. Resolving to have a look around in the morning, Gina put on her best, most grateful game face and joined the group by a small, sliding door.

Peter pushed a brass button. Soon, metallic clanging was joined by a pained screech, and the elevator door opened. It was a creaky, decorative affair of polished, carved wood and fanciful swirls of gilded metal grating. Its size indicated its date and original purpose of transporting no more than three people at a time. Gina rolled her eyes.

"I'll take the stairs."

"No you won't," Peter hissed, grabbing her shoulder. "We're staying together."

Taking multiple trips of people and luggage would take time. She glanced at Vera, who nodded. "We're sharing rooms, too," she said. "They had only three left."

"Okay. Thank you." Gina followed her into the rattling cage and out, down a hallway with opulent yet threadbare carpets and small, crystal chandeliers that cast inadequate light from the tall ceilings.

Vera unlocked the dark, heavy door with a large gothic key. The room itself would have been generous enough, had the owners not crammed four beds into a space that was designed to accommodate only two.

"This looks like a dormitory," Vera said. "And look – this furniture's so old, it would be considered antique back in the States."

"It's pretty," Gina said, giving it the benefit of doubt. The novelty of the Old World hadn't lost its shine just yet. "The ceilings are so tall, and it's so old-fashioned, and I am so tired I don't give a damn where I sleep tonight, as long as it's better than the car."

They changed into something a bit more comfortable, made use of the miniature bathroom, and slipped into their respective beds.

The lights were off. Gina took a cleansing breath, ready to drift into much-needed sleep.

A monster gurgled in the dark.

"What was that?" Vera whispered.

"I dunno." Gina's voice was a faint croak. She heard it too – a sound as though somebody stifled a burp.

"I'll check it out. You stay here." Gina heard the slither of the worn bed sheets and the old bedcovers.

A zipper gave a faint, metallic zing.

The click of Vera's gun slide was a familiar sound by now.

"Vera?"

"Shh."

Gina raised her head a bit. Vera's silhouette, crouched, crab-walked between the crowded beds all the way to the bathroom. En-suite toilets and showers must have been an afterthought in a place as old as this, because the bathroom had a plastic accordion screen instead of a proper door.

A sudden light blinded her.

Vera held a flashlight in one hand, her Glock in the other, wrist crossed. A kick - the plastic accordion door sighed and clattered to the worn parquet floor.

Few beats of silence elapsed as Vera gasped for breath. "No one's here," she said. There was a sheepish quality to her voice, and through her raucous heartbeat, Gina felt a giggle bubble up her throat. "Cockroach! There's a cockroach!"

Gina vaulted off her creaky bed and hurried to Vera's side. The black insects scurried away from the beam of Vera's tactical flashlight.

They locked gazes as though deciding whether to be disgusted or amused, when the sound gurgled from the bathroom again. This time it was accompanied by a strong sulphuric smell.

"Our room is possessed by an angry toilet god," Gina quipped. Vera turned the lights back on, ejected the round from the chamber of her gun, and fed it back into the magazine. She stashed the weapon under her pillow.

"Would you turn off the lights, please?" she said. "I'm sure there were cockroaches in other hotels where I have stayed. I absolutely refuse to be flustered over this."

"Okay," Gina said. "But what about the angry toilet god?"

"You figure out whether it's a good topic for your thesis." Vera yawned. "I'm going to sleep."

THE MORNING revealed the tired grandeur of their surroundings with merciless abandon. Gina rolled out of her bed to find cigarette burns in the quilted cover, something she'd been too tired to notice the night before. The angry toilet god groaned his irritating song of malice every time either she or Vera used the sink. She eyed the miniature shower stall.

"I see you are thinking about it, too," Vera said. "They do seem to have hot water."

"When do you think we'll be in Vienna?"

"It's about two hundred and fifty kilometers. Figure four hours. Maybe more, if the weather's bad." Vera stashed away her clothes and zipped her small suitcase shut.

"So we'll be in Vienna by tonight," Gina said, mostly because Vera was ready to go. "I guess I'll survive."

"I think you may not survive if you try to shower here. If their system smells this bad with us only using the sink, can you imagine what gallons of hot water would do to it?"

Gina shrugged. "I've slept in a shepherd's hut in Macedonia. There was enough hay, and there was a well right outside. I can survive a few more days without cleaning up."

THEY DESCENDED the wide staircase. Vera followed her nose past the carved reception desk, over polished marble floors, and straight into an opulent ballroom. The men saved seats for them by the two tables they took up. They were halfway done with their meal. Noting the unoccupied seat next to Peter, Vera wove her way through the maze of mostly empty tables and settled down next to him.

"How's the food?"

"Better than the beds," he said and bit off a piece of bread and cheese. "How did you sleep?"

"Well, after I performed an armed search of the bathroom to make sure no one was hiding in it, not bad."

Peter raised his eyebrows. "Armed? Really?"

She shrugged and poured herself a cup of coffee.

"Was anybody in there?"

"Just cockroaches."

Peter threw his head back in a burst of laughter. It drew attention, and Vera poked him with her elbow. "I'll go see if the food is unaffected by the angry toilet god." Her gaze stopped at their neighboring table and she paused. "Aww, how sweet. Look, Gina's helping Zhenia get his breakfast."

With just a corner of her vision, she noted the way Peter's jaw tightened. She gave him a benevolent smile. "Can I get you anything?"

"No. I'm good. I want to be on the road in fifteen."

The tension in the air was almost palpable. There was Vera, smug that Gina was no longer fixated on her husband. There was Peter, vexed that his shine seemed to have worn off.

Their deal of him indulging in extramarital sexcapades included Vera's lack of criticism. She found the agreement she'd made years ago harder to keep, and Peter's roving eye did put her under more strain than ever before. Yet she loved him, and he loved her.

"You're a fascinating, tough woman," he whispered in her hear. "I probably don't deserve you."

She forced a smile. In years past, these words would've produced a happy glow that carried her through the day, if not the week. Five years of marriage later, his compliments were just words. Clear water falling into a cup of charred coffee.

He was right. He probably didn't deserve her.

Yet here they were, in the fairy-tale ballroom full of Venetian mirrors and frou-frou scrollwork on the walls, like from a princess movie. The air between them was charged with something uncomfortably close to resentment.

She didn't know how it could have happened, how did their path twist and turn and threatened to split up ahead. Vera stood and stretched to shake of the feeling of uncertainty.

"No, sit, go ahead and eat," Peter told Vera quickly, and in that moment, his voice was almost tender. "Take as long as you need. I'm not going anywhere."

If it only were so, she thought as she reached for a piece of poppy-filled pastry.

GINA'S EXCITEMENT at getting to see Hungary waned with every truck they passed. A fine mist of kicked-up rainwater hazed over the road, diminishing visibility and slowing traffic to a crawl.

She wished she was driving and had a measure of control over their safety. Peter's old driver was behind the wheel and Peter rode shotgun next to him. Gina sat behind the driver's seat, as before, and Zhenia leaned into the padded vinyl seat next to her. They abandoned all pretense of not being a group of two cars that travelled together, and the old license plates resumed their rightful position on the fronts and the backs of each car. Even the dirty car, camouflaged with Vera's toiletries and river mud, looked black and shiny after the rain. Fake passports were stowed away, and new identities took residence in the men's pockets.

It occurred to her that this identity she knew, Vera and Peter Christoff, might have been a fake one as well. On the other hand, she knew Vera's name from the world of art. She had published various academic articles and was no stranger to the guest lecturer circuit. Vera Christoff was probably real. Gina wasn't so sure about the others.

Gina's thoughts turned to her injured travel companion as she leaned her head against the back of the seat, observing him on the sly.

Zhenia was about her age, or maybe a few years older. His face had an ordinary, unassuming symmetry under the scruffy growth that was untouched by a razorblade since the car accident. His right arm was the one with a cast and in the sling.

111

She smiled. Zhenia was probably right-handed, and he didn't feel comfortable asking his companions to shave him. The group had, at first, seemed like a tight-knit unit of best buds who'd happened to land the same job. Guys like that would feel at ease with one another. Casual and trusting. One needed to trust the other in order to accept a shave. Yet Zhenia opted for a bad-boy look that might garner him unwanted attention at the border.

Zhenia turned toward her.

She was caught staring. There was that temptation to duck under the seat and disappear from the world for the foreseeable future, but then Zhenia smiled, and she found it was easy to smile right back at him. His eyes were cornflower blue, almost crystalline in their brightness. She had noticed specks of hazel rimming the iris – more so on the right than the left side – but the dim light didn't betray his eye color now, and Gina didn't have to worry about drowning in his depths.

She'd noticed his eyes at breakfast earlier, and when Gina helped him carry food to the table, he nodded his thanks and uttered a shy "Spasibo" just as the other two men at the table snorted and elbowed each another. When Gina poured him coffee and asked whether he wanted milk or sugar in a heavily accented Russian, they became the targets of significant looks from their tablemates.

Presently, Gina pulled a bottle of pills out of her pocket and extended it toward him. She cocked her eyebrow, and he nodded and raised two fingers. Gina dispensed two pink and white capsules. They sat on her palm and he fumbled for them with the fingers of his left hand. There was a lot more skin contact than she expected. She remained still and enjoyed Zhenia's warmth against her hand. Soon she would go her own way and he'd turn to whatever new arms-dealing, smuggling project Peter Christoff desired.

Hungary flew by in a dark grey mist of rain and fields and electric high-voltage lines. She expected picturesque towns, and horses, and women in embroidered costumes working in the fields she had seen in books and travel brochures, but there was nothing. Just the fallow winter fields and sheets of driving rain, and the trucks that emerged from the mist like dangerous whales upon the flat and endless sea.

She leaned back and closed her eyes. As she drifted off to sleep, her mind dredged up an image of a stack of old Soviet RPGs on a wooden loading pallet, and the sleek and entirely menacing form of a stray Stinger missile.

A HAND ON her knee woke her up. She chose not to shake it off - Zhenia was getting adventurous. She leaned into his warmth some more and smiled, cheek against his shoulder imprinted with the quilted pattern of his waterproof jacket. He pressed his thigh into hers, and she smiled.

"Gina!" Peter hissed, and now the hand shook her knee. Gina opened her eyes and saw Peter Christoff turned toward her from the front end of the car.

"We're at the border. Get your papers out." He didn't say anything after that. Zhenia squeezed her thigh encouragingly. She straightened up and moved back to the middle of her seat. The hand was gone, and Zhenia's warmth was gone, and she realized she'd slept all the way through Hungary and didn't get to see any of it. Well, except for the roach hotel.

"I'm on it." She dug for her passport in her backpack. Within minutes, they were in yet another restricted zone, their passports were examined and stamped, and only minutes after that, they entered Austria.

It wasn't even dark yet. She expected a much longer trip. "Peter, what time is it?"

"Four," he said, not even glancing at his watch. "We'll find a place to stay in Vienna, then we'll have our last dinner together, and get you home to Italy."

She didn't answer, thinking that Italy wasn't really her home. She went to school in Ravenna, true, but she checked in every so often with her professors, she handed in papers and grant proposals, and as long as her advisor got a steady stream of productive work out of her, she was left to do pretty much as she pleased.

It struck her as odd that she ran into gun-runners in a place where she expected to find art smugglers. The more she thought about it, the more sense it made. The Balkans were the crossroads between the exotic, spice-laden cultures of Asia Minor and the safe and staid Europe. If she had a truck, she could carry all kinds of goods in it. A route demands goods, and it made a weird sort of sense that an established route of smugglers would transport weapons as well as ancient church relics into the hands of the highest bidder.

The road hummed under the wheels of their car, the rain hissing on the pavement. As they forged their way through the wet silence, the thought of ancient routes remained etched in her mind.

THEY CROSSED into Austria as smoothly as they did into Hungary. Another rolled-down window, another stamp in her passport, although she was glad that she didn't have to hunker down under Peter's overcoat this time around. The rain subsided and only a wet road reminded her of the snowstorm that had chased them out of the Serbian mountains and that pursued them, melting into impotent rain, hissing across the plains of the Magyars. They passed vast areas of open land, with trees on the right side and tilled fields on the left.

The traffic thickened – of course, the airport. Gina took comfort in the sight of the large machines taking off and landing. It was a sign of civilization, one that had been a rare sight over the last few months. Trucks gave way to sedans as the road forged on.

She peered through the wet and murky air outside the car. The Danube must have been here somewhere. She'd seen it on the map, and figured they would drive by it except there was nothing but the barren trees and fallow fields, and cars.

"Eww, what is that smell?" The words were out of her mouth before she could apply her customary filters. The stench was alien yet familiar, evoking the feel of home, yet repulsive nonetheless.

"Refineries," Peter said with a wry grin. "Don't you come from New Jersey? I thought you'd be used to that kind of a thing."

"Oh." Now that she had a name for it, the pungent, acrid, organic smell drew memories of strip malls and traffic and pizza. "We didn't live in Elizabeth, but yeah. You couldn't live in Northern Jersey and escape the smell at least once in a while."

Then it was gone, the odor replaced by Peter's breath mints, and the road carried them past residential buildings surrounded by old trees. She saw a group of open stores wink away through the receding light of the day, and realized that this might well be the first mall she had seen in several months.

Traffic thickened some more as they wove their way on A4 into the heart of the old Hapsburg Empire. The highway gave way to large boulevards lined with soaring buildings. Every doorway and window and mantelpiece was embellished in expert stonework that proclaimed the wealth of the Austria-Hungary. Trees lined the boulevards, keeping the traffic away from the wide sidewalks.

People walked in the rain, carrying umbrellas and shopping bags. It must have been just past quitting time. By now, Gina's nose was plastered to the cold glass of the car window, halfway in love and to hell with dignity. Rome was imposing and Florence was amazing, but no city was as baroque, as orderly, and as stately as the formerly imperial capital of Wien.

CHAPTER 14

THEY PULLED up to a building which was fluffy with a surfeit of carved stone decorations, and imposing in its size. As such, it anchored the end of a small square with true imperial arrogance. Its entryway was as big as Gina's parent's house, and two staircases curved up and met on a terrace in front of the door. Their carved stone banisters looked like the curved spines of sleek sea creatures, and their upswept shape formed a hidden, intimate space on the street level.

The water fountain placed there was perfect and, somehow, inevitable. Its basin was empty for the winter and a naked brass dryad stood in the middle, apparently unconcerned by the smell of snow in the air.

"We're here," Peter prodded her. "You'll have enough time to look around later." His tone was amused, but his expression held tender understanding. "I take it you have never been to Vienna before?"

"No. I figured it would be like Paris, but it's not. It's more… just more full of itself. Is the whole city like this?"

Peter humored her with a smile. "Not really, although the locals would like you to believe that. Come, I'll get your luggage."

Gina jumped out of the car and hoisted her own backpack over one shoulder and picked up her duffel in the other hand. "I'm fine, really, but thank you. I'll be okay." Her eyes drifted toward Zhenia and the way he had trouble getting out of the car. She watched him pick up a duffle bag with his good hand, and was just about to offer to carry it when Peter cleared his throat and gave her a piercing look.

"But…"

"No." He shook his head. Then he sidled up close to her and whispered in her ear. "Don't cut his balls off. He feels useless enough as it is."

"Oh." She paused. "Thanks." Their eyes met, Peter's molten-chocolate brown warm and inviting, and she thought back to the sultry promise of their kiss in Zabljak. They had stood as close as this back then.

Even closer.

Right now, Peter's eyes had a wistful look, like a boy whose face was pressed against a candy store display case. It was her turn to cough a bit. The store was closed.

"You sound like you need some tea!" Peter recovered his footing with the grace of a professional hustler. "Here, let's secure our rooms and we can meet downstairs. There is a lovely café with the best Viennese desserts."

"Are you ready to go?" Vera's voice, sharp and brittle like a crushed Christmas ornament, broke the unwelcome tension. She picked up her suitcase and strode on, leading the way up the stairs and toward the imposing brass door.

GINA HAD a room all to herself. The two twin beds were pressed together to form a bed for a couple, European-style. The room had a high ceiling and was infused with the waning light that filtered through the sheer curtains from the outside even at dusk. Space, air, and sleek, modern décor.

She laughed aloud at the unweighted feeling of space and her sudden ability to take a very deep breath. After harrowing days on the road, she had privacy, a lovely balcony in the chill air outside, and her own bathroom. The same amenities as she had had a short driving distance from the war zone had felt like a prison then, yet now they were palatial. Now she was free.

Gone was the cast-iron tub she'd expected. This place had been remodeled recently, if the large soaking tub and new tiles were anything to go by. She fingered the plush terry-cotton towels with a sense of wonder. With towels such as these, the hotel surely saw a good bit of American trade. She, along with her fellow countrymen, had always found the thin, woven bath towels of Europe an irritating challenge.

Not today, though. Gina glanced at her watch. She had well over an hour before everyone was scheduled to meet downstairs. She plugged the tub and turned the water on. The complimentary toiletries smelled like orange blossom and a hint of something else, and Gina took a deep breath over the gushing faucet as she squeezed in some of the bath gel. Then she ran off to the other room and rummaged for a change of clothes.

Nothing was clean, and if she washed things, they might not dry till the next day, let alone dinner. The hotel information packet had an English-language section, though, and in it she found laundry information. She picked the least dirty of her clothes to wear tonight, stuffed the rest into a laundry bag, and called the extension in the portfolio.

"Guten Abend," a female voice on the other side said.

"Do you speak English?" Gina's response was no response at all, but experience had taught her to survey her challenges upfront.

"A little," the woman said in a heavily accented voice. "How can I help you?"

"I need to do the laundry."

There was a beat of silence, and it stretched uncomfortably while the sound of running water continued from the bathroom.

"Wash clothes," Gina said. Then she repeated it in Italian.

"Ach, clothes! Ja. What is your room number?"

With the information exchanged, Gina shoved a bag of laundry outside her door, locked up, and ran to rescue her bath. The tub was full and the excess of hot water was going out the emergency overflow drain. She turned the water off, tested the temperature, and lowered herself in slowly enough not to cause a flood.

Heavenly. Absolutely divine. She had not had a shower or a bath since Zabljak, and even though that had been several days ago, it felt like forever. The warmth soaked into her bones and the kinks and aches of travel dissolved in the buoyant caress of orange blossoms.

She washed her hair. Appalled by the murky color of her bath, she let the water out and refilled the tub anew. Off with the sweat and the stress and the fear - she rinsed off the silt from the River Morava and the road grime she picked up from the cars. She scoured every bit of Serbian countryside and purged the memory of Szeged's angry toilet god from her mind. This was heaven, and she would stay as long as she could. Immersed, afloat, adrift, soaking the Balkans off her body, she closed her eyes in bliss.

An image of a Stinger missile invaded her mind. A dark, sleek shape with angular wings, in a crate with its launcher. Transferred from the trunk of the black sedan into the back of the moving van.

For the first time, she heard the words Peter Christoff had said clearly in her mind. It was as though her understanding of Russian had risen several levels over the last few days and, now that she had the luxury to recall all he had said, every word was clear.

"There is more where these came from."

PETER WAS PLEASED with his choice of a restaurant, which was only one street over. He took in the stained glass chandeliers and the old, dark paneling on the walls. The chairs were plain wood with curved, Biedermeier-style legs, but the tables were covered in pristine white and the smells from the kitchen promised a pleasant meal.

The waiter pulled the chair out for Vera. Not to miss an opportunity, Peter turned to pull a chair for Gina. Yet she was already seated, on Zhenia's good side and with Zhenia's good arm on the backrest of Gina's chair.

His jaw tightened. Vera met his eyes from across the long table. He expected anger, or the weird possessiveness she had been nurturing for the last year or so. Yet there was only her gentle, professional smile. It was directed at him, with just a hint of pity in her eyes.

Pity.

He recoiled. He was Peter Christoff and they had a deal. He got to enjoy other women as long as he would love her the way he loved none of them. Yet now, this pretty young thing showed interest in his bodyguard, and his crippled, idiotic bodyguard must've been taking lessons from Peter over the last two months, because he sure as hell had pulled Gina's chair out for her.

He considered firing the man, except Zhenia came recommended by one of Uncle Ilya's friends. This did not make him trustworthy – merely

119

acceptable. Uncle Ilya should've been here in person, except for the small detail of his leukemia. His sons should have stepped up, but their language skills were limited.

Peter would have appreciated Oleg and Alexi at his back.

They didn't always get along and their childhood jealousies still resonated through their adult relationships, but they were kin, and they all knew they would have each other's back. Had they been here, there would have been no need to hire Zhenia and his friend. His glance at Zhenia brought Peter back to the problem of getting into Gina's bed. Her lack of interest made him feel older than his late thirties.

"What will you have?" Vera asked him as she perused the menu. "The usual?"

He realized she had been helping the others read the menu while the waiter was standing at attention, ready to take down his order.

"A schnitzel with spaetzle and a cucumber salad," he said, relying on his favorite. "And a beer." This led to a discussion of what was on tap. They all had pretty much the same thing.

"Sorry for spacing out," he said when the waiter left. Vera only nodded.

"It's okay. You are understandably distracted."

"Distracted?" He didn't like where this was going.

"Defeat doesn't suit you."

He shrugged. "Win some, lose some. There are other fish in the sea." Yet the barb found its home under the thick armor he had cultivated over the years and he found it difficult to just let it slide. A gulp of bitter beer washed down the bad taste the conversation left in his mouth, and he turned to Gina.

"So, Gina. What do you think of Vienna so far?"

THE AFTER-DINNER conversation took them into coffee and aperitif and dessert. Peter observed his wife and Gina Francesca Migliore and the way their interests and conversation patterns interweaved. They had so much in common. The enjoyment Vera took in her mentorship role was apparent.

"Have you considered talking to the fences?" Vera asked.

"I don't really know who resells stolen artifacts," Gina said. "I know they pop up in smaller galleries, or in private collection, and the chain of their provenance is broken by then. The galleries never say where they got this vase or that statuette. It's as though…" She paused, searching for words. "It's as though there was this steady stream of goods. The turnover is solid so the supply needs to be pretty regular. At least, that's how I see it."

She paused uncertainly, but when Vera nodded, she continued. "Which means, either there's a huge warehouse full of ancient artifacts somewhere and whoever dug them up is releasing them bit by bit, or there's a steady series of digs. I'd guess the former, though. It makes more sense logistically."

"It does. And don't forget, if a farmer finds coins or an old amphora in the fields, selling them to a private dealer is a lot more profitable than going though the state-mandated process, which would get him just a small finder's fee. And you saw the Balkans. The people in the countryside don't have much. Few hundred dollars are a fortune to them." Peter watched Vera moisten her lips in her beer. She never drank much, a fact that his family found confusing. She licked the foam off and turned to Peter.

"Do you know anyone Gina could contact? She's interested in tracking down the sites of the original finds, not in reporting people."

He looked at Gina with renewed interest. She was young and energetic, and she'd shown perseverance and grit throughout their adventure. Vera seemed happy with her grasp on her art and history – and he did just happen to know a man who bought almost anything from almost anyone. Including stolen artifacts.

Including old Soviet RPGs.

"This could get dangerous." His tone was serious and he held Gina's gaze with unflinching intensity. "These are not nice people."

"They are looking to profit, though," she said. "I might have something to sell, too. Nothing major. A few coins, maybe."

"No." Peter shook his head. "Once it comes out you're dealing, you'll be discredited in the art world, and you won't be able to explain that you were working undercover and on your own. Too many people have tried to use that excuse as a cover for massive art theft." He turned the empty glass in his fingers. The beer was gone, and only a hint of foam adhered to the curved walls now. It was gone, like Gina would be gone, marking his life with her passage in an attractive, albeit temporary way.

"There's a guy I know on Cyprus. He'll talk to you if I ask him, but don't expect miracles."

HER STOMACH was full of good food, she was clean and dressed in laundered clothing, and the bed she was in was soft and clean. Its white bedclothes rustled with good cotton, and Gina had warmed her nest just enough to really resent a knock on her door. She bit back a frustrated groan, heaved herself out of bed, and padded to the door. She looked through the peephole.

"Gina?" Peter Christoff's voice sounded almost clear through the door. She opened.

"I was in bed already."

He gave her a warm smile and reached for her hand. "I figured. Do you have everything you need?"

She felt his thumb circle over the inside of her wrist. Only a few days back she would have welcomed his advances, but those few days felt like an eternity now.

And she really liked his wife. Dr. Vera Christoff was a woman of substance, and despite any kind of an arrangement Peter claimed they had, Gina noticed the pained expression on Vera's face as Peter did his gentleman act.

"It was very kind of you to give me a ride," she said.

"I've really grown fond of your company, Gina."

"I appreciate the meals and the emergency cash. Give me an address where I can mail a check. I'll settle with you as soon as I get back to Ravenna."

Peter frowned. "There's no need. A gift is a gift – please do not try to return it." He lifted her fingers to his lips and kissed their top.

She pulled her hand free and crossed her arms across her chest. "I am not going to sleep with you, Peter." Her declaration was firm and clear.

Peter Christoff, a man who was used to getting his way, straightened up with an expression of disbelief.

"I won't be a kept woman," she said, and felt no small amount of satisfaction in addressing the tension between them. "You're attractive and pleasant, but that doesn't mean I want be one of your love-em-and-leave-em girls. What's most important, though, is I don't want to be the cause of Vera's hurt feelings." Her voice trailed off to a softer tone, but her feet didn't move.

Peter Christoff was still standing out in the hallway.

"She and I, we have a deal. She won't mind. We've been doing this for years."

"She too would mind. You're a really nice guy, Peter, and I appreciate you giving me that contact for Zeno in Cyprus, but… I can't. It has all kinds of wrong written all over it."

His expression wavered. "A nice guy? I'm not a nice guy. Calling me a nice guy is a kiss of death. I thought you liked me."

"And I still do. Good night, Peter."

CHAPTER 15

GINA WALKED in a direction she hoped was mostly north. The art museum should have been north of the hotel, and she should have already passed it, except she just wasn't sure anymore. Every building in Vienna was opulent enough to be a museum.

The backpack was comfortable on her back, but the strap of her duffel was digging into her shoulder and she felt all steamed up under her jacket despite the chill of the morning. She leaned against a lamppost and dumped her duffel on the ground. Casting a wary look – no one was sneaking up - she pulled the small tourist map out of her pocket and unfolded it again. It was the kind she got at the hotel's reception desk just after breakfast, and before she ran into Peter and Vera and all their men.

Their parting had been awkward. They already had each other's contact information, Peter reiterated that he would thwart any effort at being repaid for anything, and Vera invited her to look her up when they both returned to the States. Gina shook everybody's hand and let her fingers linger in Zhenia's warm palm. Something about him piqued her interest. Zhenia had a secret – and it wasn't just his pretty blue eyes with flecks of golden hazel - and Gina wanted to find out what it was. Hell, she wouldn't mind being Zhenia's secret, if even for a short while.

Their eyes met and they smiled at each other with more than politeness required, and before she knew it, Gina had found herself on the streets of Vienna.

SHE LOOKED at the map and then glanced at the enameled street sign that was attached to the building on the corner. Looking for the museum turned out to be useless. The same all neo-baroque, ornate style buildings smelled of old money, and history, and privilege. Despite her awe and best intentions, she began to tune out the statues and friezes and ornate porticoes, and walked on in search of a landmark she could actually find on the map.

"Schottenring." The name rolled off her tongue in a way that was both familiar and foreign. It was a long street with lanes divided by rows of trees.

She thought it looked familiar. The structure of the naked branches and the perspective of the old buildings reminded her of a painting she had seen a long time ago. The boulevard was vast, and she followed it, because she was not lost.

Just like in Macedonia.

She was exploring, and she was yet to find where, exactly, she was. *That wasn't the same as lost*, she reminded herself as she walked on. The Schottenring ended in a mess of green parks and a ring and what looked like a bus turnaround, and the nearby street sign informed her that she was now on Universitätsring. She saw a complex of large and stately buildings to her oblique left, and a park with a church – obviously a church and not a museum - to her oblique right.

Those features and those names were big enough to show up on a freebie hotel map, surely.

She had been heading west. This was a surprise to her, and she chalked it to the fact that the murky skies hid the sun, and she was unable to orienteer the way she would have in the sunny Balkans.

She plotted her course, hoisted her duffle once again, and set out north – or at least she hoped that, this time, it was the real north – on Währinger Strasse. The countless blocks of hard pavement echoed in her sore feet when the street veered to the right past yet another lush city park. Leaf mold mingled with the exhaust of diesel-powered cars in the crisp winter air at the next intersection, and her hands felt cold even tucked inside her pockets. None of that mattered, though, because the street sign on the next building said "Boltzmanngasse."

The U.S. Embassy was located further down this street.

125

The street soon turned into a pedestrian zone of sorts, like a courtyard where only the privileged were allowed to park. The U.S. Embassy building was as large and imperial as any of the complexes she had passed in her morning wanderings. She was hungry and tired and cold, and the sight of the American flag stirring in the breeze spurred her on. Small snowflakes began to dance before her face and she laughed at her fortuitous timing. The entry to the U.S. Embassy building was as imposing as any in Vienna, but all she felt was welcome and relief. She pushed the large door open and walked in from the cold.

GINA LOOKED around. The lobby was large and cavernous, and she had trouble picking out where to go next. Warm illumination from incandescent bulbs mingled with the pale, insipid light that poured in through tall windows framed by stately velvet curtains. She caught glimmers of gold-tone brass, and of crystal prisms and the lovely, soft foliage in planters by the stairs.

"Wilkommen."

Gina followed the sound of the stern, female voice. A semi-circular desk stood in her way. The American flag right behind it lent bright color to the interior. The receptionist sat behind the desk and Gina realized she was being studied. The woman, dressed in a black and tan business suit, was looking her up and down through her gold-rimmed glasses. There were guards in uniform, but they stood inside and Gina was amazed that she had not noticed them right away.

"Guten tag. Hello. Do you speak English?" Gina said as she worked to shake off the daze of her trip.

She gave Gina a professional smile. "Yes, I do. How may I help you?" Her English sounded American.

Gina contemplated the question. She knew she needed help getting back to Florence, but she also needed some help in relaying sensitive information, and she wasn't going to tell the receptionist and all these random strangers about an arms deal she saw go down over in Serbia. She made a show of blowing on her pale hands while thinking hard.

"I just got out of Serbia," she said. "I got kind of stuck down there, and somebody gave me a ride up here. I need help figuring out how to get back to where I need to go."

"Are you a U.S. citizen?" The receptionist asked, and when Gina nodded, the woman nodded to one of the guards. "Please take her upstairs and have her fill out a form."

A Marine in a full dress uniform escorted Gina up a marble staircase and to the right. The bottom of the stairs was guarded by another pair of Marines in their dress blues, with white covers on top of their Marine haircuts. Gina let her eye stray just for the scenery when she realized there was something familiar about them. It wasn't so much that they reminded her of her cousin Dom. It was their carriage – the way they stood, the way they owned their space – she'd seen it before. More importantly, she had seen it recently.

She thought of Zhenia.

He owned space around him like that, even while in pain. Gina thought maybe he used to be in the Soviet special forces. Service was still compulsory over there and she figured those guys might have similar body language.

Then she wondered whether soldiers the world over had the same body language.

Then she thought the Marine walking her down the corridor might have noticed her ogling him, and she quickly looked ahead.

They walked down a long corridor, whose ceiling was supported by stately arches and whose walls were punctuated by evenly spaced doorways. She noticed the murmur of voices rise and fall from behind the doors as they passed, and she wished they could have at least paused so she could identify the languages spoken.

When her escort knocked on a doorframe, Gina was almost disappointed. The embassy was a fascinating place, full of activity, and she would have loved to know what was going on and why. The Marine pushed an open door until it gaped.

"Right in here, Miss." He gave her a smile she was glad to return.

"Thank you," she said, and turned her attention to the room.

"COME RIGHT IN." The words came from the man that sat behind the desk. He was only a few years older than she was, and he remained seated as she entered the room. It struck her as boorish after all the old-fashioned courtesies of Peter Christoff, and she had to school her face into an expression that was at least neutral.

"How can I help you?" he asked without introducing himself. Gina considered her lengthy trek in the weather outside. If anything, she would sit here for quite a while.

"First of all, if you don't mind, may I use your restroom?"

"Of course." He heaved himself from a leather executive chair and walked Gina out the door. "It's down to the right."

The cramped bathroom spoke of a bygone era, with a flush tank mounted under the ceiling and a flush chain with a painted porcelain pull and the smallest little hand-sink she had ever seen. The place might have been cramped, but it was a lot better than a stack of logs by the river. She even got to wash her hands. Ah, civilization.

The man ushered her back into the small office. She took her time sitting down in the stuffed leather chair, examining her environment. The obligatory flag and the portrait of President Clinton, and various certificates in frames on the wall.

The office bore no stamp of personal preference. No papers, no files, no books. Certainly no family photos. The whitewashed walls were cast in gray shadows, and snow swirled on eddies of air outside the window.

"So," he started, once he examined her passport and the short form she filled out. "Your name is Gina Francesca Migliore. Is that correct?"

"Yes."

And so it went, down every single item on the droll official form, until she felt rather small under his scrutiny and her shoulders began to tighten up. Just then, he sent her a small smile.

"That sounds like quite an adventure, getting stuck south of Dubrovnik. How did you get all the way to Vienna, again?" His tone of voice didn't go with that smile he gave her, and taken altogether, he looked like an arrogant prick. Gina's sense of wrongness grew to alarming proportions. She couldn't quite put her finger on what bothered her so much, but she felt her enthusiasm for cooperation retreat under its turtle shell.

"I already gave you the basics." Gina squared her shoulders and looked him straight in the eye. "And I don't really know you. All I know is you said you are an assistant to the cultural attaché, and I don't see how this information would do you any good. I do have some things to say, but I don't think I want to say them to you."

She watched his posture tighten, as though he were a predator who scented the lingering smell of dinner on the air. Instantly, she was on guard.

"Why not me?" he said.

She took care to soften her tone. "You were kind enough to offer me a loan to get back to Florence, which is great and I'll be happy to accept it, but... " She thought of her brother and his barely functioning arm. Her mind was flooded with his tales of Mogadishu and the Red Sea and the bite of the desert wind in the eyes. She also thought back to the words he'd say when her incessant questions got to be too much. *"You don't have the need to know."*

"You don't have the need to know." The words flew out of her mouth all by themselves, arrogant and smooth. Before she had a chance to regret them, the man across the desk from her quirked his eyebrows and bit his lip.

"Excuse me for a second." He picked up the telephone and dialed an extension. She heard the faint echo of somebody picking it up on the other side.

"I have a young lady here, Walt. She has something to say, but she says I don't have the need to know." He smiled as he listened to the few words of response. "Okay. We'll wait for you here." Then he hung up and turned toward Gina. "The boss is coming."

THE SILENCE OF waiting thickened the air. Gina sat up straight and leaned into her chair. She needed the contact of the firm wood and padded leather backrest.

Needed to feel her feet grounded on the polished wooden floor.

The man across the desk sat as though stillness was an old companion. He was tall and slender and his dark hair was cut short. His face was shaven smooth, and his gray suit fit him so well, Gina figured it was bespoke. And she realized, as suddenly as though she was struck by lightning, that the suit was the outlier. The bespoke suit and its exceptionally fine material reeked of wrongness, of not belonging. She didn't trust him because of that. Gina knew how much her grandmother charged for custom-made suits back in the States, and she didn't see how a man on a government salary could afford one.

He smiled.

She looked out the window. The world outside darkened and the snowflakes danced the mating dance of bright moths, illuminated by the outdoor lights that flooded the façade of the embassy. She felt trapped, glued to her chair like a figurine inside a snowball, and she didn't want to look at the man in the gray suit. Assistant to whatever or whoever. A gofer who wore a suit with a price tag of a small, used vehicle.

THE STILLNESS WAS broken by the sound of shoes – men's shoes, not heels – scuffing the parquet floors. She sat with her back to the door. This was bound to be the boss.

Gina turned away from the window and stood and faced the open door, and as she did so, a man filled its frame. He was in his fifties and his graying hair was receding into a widow's peak. He wore silver-tone wire rim glasses and his face was sallow and jowly. Yet there was a sparkle of amusement in his deep-set eyes. He didn't slow down as he walked all the way up to Gina and offered his hand.

"So you're the one," he said, and she shook his hand because it was expected.

"So, Gina, you tell me the assistant to the attaché has no need to know." The familiarity of his address irked her. Neither of the men had bothered to introduce themselves, and this old fart was trying to treat her like a kid who was caught skipping school. She pumped his hand again before releasing it.

"That's right, Walt." There. Turnabout was fair play.

130

Walt shot a sour look at the man in the grey, tailored suit. "Maybe you don't have a need to know after all."

Ah. So his name really was Walt. Probably Walter. She wasn't supposed to know that, and now she did. The sensation of having won a small contest warmed Gina from within.

"Since we are on a first-name basis, Walt, how about you and I step out somewhere private, and I'll give you a brief rundown. Then you can decide what to do with this mess."

The man in the gray suit cleared his throat in that "look at me, and look at me now" way, but Walt didn't, and neither did Gina. They stood, the chair still partially between them. Gina felt the weight of Walt's measuring gaze and returned it right back. There he was, taller than she was, and kind of broad in the shoulders, like a guy who used to play football years ago. He had a half a beer keg where his six-pack used to be. His suit was navy and had a dark green stripe and it hung off him like something he bought on a Black Friday sale, and his tie was polyester and its knot was a lot looser than it was supposed to be.

Gina saw a man on a government salary who didn't give a flying fuck what she thought of him. He reminded her of her crazy uncle Ernie, who had a moonshine still on the roof of his apartment building in Hoboken and who bribed the super with a cut of his production every year. She gave an infinitesimal nod.

Walt broke the silence. "John. Get out of here and close the door."

"YOUR STOMACH sounds pretty loud, kid," Walt continued as he picked up the phone. "Brenda. I'm in Room Two. Could you have the kitchen bring some sandwiches for two? And coffee. Or tea?" He turned to Gina with his bushy eyebrows exercising like two overactive caterpillars.

"Coffee," she whispered.

"Just coffee," he said. "And something to go with it. I have a very important guest to entertain."

Gina heard an acerbic tone cut him off on the other side, but he just smiled and put the receiver in the cradle. Then he wheeled the stuffy executive chair to the side of the desk so they sat kitty-corner from one another. The barrier between them was lesser now, and for the first time in days, Gina felt like she could breathe freely enough to sigh.

"So. I am going to record this, okay? It's easier than taking notes."

She nodded.

"Tell me what happened, from the beginning."

CHAPTER 16

"Where are you staying tonight?" Walt asked as they finished. The coffee was all gone, her passport was back in her security pocket, and she still had a bit of Peter's cash warming her wallet.

"I figured I'd go to the train station. I need to check the schedules to get back to Florence. If there's a night train, I could sleep on the train. If not, I'll get a room in a cheap pension nearby."

"Okay," he nodded, and Gina thought she saw a glimmer of satisfaction. "I can help you with the train schedules, anyhow, since we keep their up-to-date charts for stranded travelers such as yourself."

"I don't feel particularly stranded," she said. "I'm here only because I had something to report. Otherwise I'd be on a train to Italy already." She didn't know why it mattered that he knew that. Maybe she wanted to see that glimmer of satisfaction again. He looked out the window, though, and picked up the telephone.

"What's the weather forecast, do you know?" He listened, grunting occasionally, then rumbled a quick "Right. Thanks," and hung up. "It's snowing. Not very much, mind you. We don't get a lot of snow cover in Vienna. However..." he leaned back until the chair creaked, and smiled. "I'd offer you a guest room if we had any, but we don't. And I want to talk to you some more, except I'll be in meetings tomorrow, and you'll be gone. So if you'd like, you can crash downstairs. There is a gym with showers, and there are some sofas where you can sleep. Surely this will be more comfortable than the train?"

She stared at him. "You want me to stay."

"Well, that's not what I said. I said I want to talk to you and I'm finding a way to do that and accommodate our mutual schedules."

"Oh." She nodded. "Sure, I can sleep on a sofa. Are there blankets?"

"We'll find you something."

HER LAUNDRY was fresh, and she used this opportunity to unpack her few possessions and place them on the sofa in the empty common room next to the embassy's basement fitness complex on the theory that it would help her luggage air out while she shook out various bits of debris. She unzipped the pockets on the duffel and emptied them. Then she did the same for her backpack. The top of the scarred, wooden coffee table were now covered with an array of notebooks, receipts, spent camera film, more receipts. Then there was the camera itself, just begging to be taken apart and cleaned. As she fished it out if its soft case, her fingers skimmed the dry, crisp paper envelope she knew so well.

Peter's letter.

She hadn't handed it over to Walt. She wasn't sure why she'd hesitated. Walt knew of the Christoffs' art-saving efforts, and he was aware of the arms deal, and he knew that Peter Christoff had been able to ease them through multiple checkpoints on a letter of passage, but something made her hold back. She still had a small scrap of paper with the name of the antiquities dealer on Cyprus, too, and she hadn't handed that over either.

Peter might have been an ass when it came to his marital relationship, but he was a kind ass, and he'd helped her out a lot. He got her out of a war zone and had spared her the indignity and danger of being stuck in a refugee camp. Tent towns, filled with desperate people and spies from the other side, were not safe places for a foreigner who had things of value on her person. She had heard the horror stories of tourists being killed for their passports alone. In the skilled hands of a crook, a photograph could be replaced. A fake US passport was a valuable commodity.

She pulled the letter out of its envelope and looked at it again. Its heavy paper and embossed seal breathed official approval and safe passage. So why was it that she felt so uneasy about it?

Spurred by a sudden impulse, she pulled out her camera. She had only two exposures left on her last roll of film, but this letter was important – so important, she was glad she wasn't in the room when Peter finally found it missing. She had wanted to take a picture of it before, but has been disturbed and had to flee Peter and Vera's room. She laid out the paper flat and propped it up against a well-lit wall. She took one picture with a flash and one without.

Footsteps prompted her to stuff the letter back in its envelope. She shoved it in her pocket. Then she tossed her camera on her pile with the rest of the gear and opened the door.

"Sorry to disturb you, kid," Walt said, rocking from his heels to his toes and back. "I just figured dinner will be served soon and you should know."

"Thanks," she said. "Where?"

"I'll take you to the cafeteria. This place is huge – no sense getting lost."

And no sense getting caught prowling around. Gina understood that her Sklenarica stunt of going up and down the trellis and breaking in was not to be repeated here. There was no need to take undue risks. She realized that her mindset was dangerously close to one of a character in a James Bond movie. Either that, or Lucille Ball.

She shook her head and smiled. "I have all this crap out so it can air out a bit. Do you figure it's safe here?"

"Yes. Ready to go?"

She nodded and left her things as they were, stopping only to wash her hands. The action seemed symbolic.

"YOU SURE have a lot of guests," Gina remarked over dessert. She knew better than to ask who these people were. Some appeared to be employees, but others looked as travel-worn as she felt.

"Vienna is the cross-roads between the East and the West," Walt said with a pensive look of a man who remembered the old days. "We used to have refugees from the Eastern Bloc come through. The mix is more diverse now, with the Balkan situation."

"I haven't seen a newspaper in days. Do you think it will settle?" Gina looked at Walt over her coffee cup. It was a nice cup, and she made sure to hold it properly, with her pinkie out. A cloud passed over Walt's face, and a few beats of silence passed before he responded.

"The Balkans have always been a powder keg. You said you have a flop in Dubrovnik, right? You heard all the languages spoken. What did you think while you were there? Didn't you feel the tension?"

"Sure I did," she retorted. "But after Italy, it felt natural. The way Italians argue all the time, and gesticulate, that's tension, too. I figured it was all just a part of that famous Mediterranean temperament."

"That would've been nice," Walt said with a laugh. "If they all argued aloud, like the Italians do, they'd have no need stabbing one another in the back in dark alleys."

The thought of blood spilled brought back the terror of almost being run off a mountain road.

"We were lucky," she said.

"Yes, you were. I'm going to one of the reading rooms, where I am allowed to smoke. It would be a pleasure if you'd join me for something to drink."

Gina felt the undercurrents of all those things Walt could have said, but didn't, about the Balkan situation. Her curiosity piqued. The din of the cafeteria receded as people filtered out, which gave them a lot less privacy. She wanted to know what he knew. She smiled. "That would be nice. Thank you."

THEY WERE in a masculine place full of books and dark furniture and leather. The indirect light gave the reading room a cozy feel, and the smoke of Walt's pipe lacked the acrid smell of cigarettes. It reminded her of incense, and she inhaled a bit of second-hand smoke just to relish a flavor that evoked nostalgia.

"You like pipe tobacco?" Walt said.

"It reminds me of my uncle," she said. "He smoked a pipe till my aunt made him give it up."

"Aunts are like that."

136

"I think the two of you would get along." She smiled, not adding that they would get along over a bottle of hooch in a covert still shed on a roof of an apartment building, with the glow of New York City just on the horizon. She sipped her whiskey instead of saying they would get along because both of them were kind of nuts.

He looked over his glass and puffed on his pipe again. "That was pretty crazy, following that guy down the trellis like that."

She shrugged.

"Did you like him?"

Gina felt a wave of heat rush up her face, and tried for a sip of whiskey to hide it, but the stinging liquid made its way down the wrong pipe and she burst into a fit of cough. Walt handed her a bar napkin, and she nodded her thanks and worked on her breathing for a little bit.

"No shame in liking a guy," he said after a while. "I'd just be curious in knowing what pushed your button about him. What made you follow him like that."

Gina thought back to when she met Peter Christoff in Podgorica. The men, the guns, the money.

"He has resources," she said slowly, thinking it all through. "Driving through Europe with three cars, all modified, with weapons that are probably illegal. My understanding is that guns are frowned upon over here." She saw him nod and thought some more before she continued. "His wife. I like her – I like her a lot, actually – but nobody normal has the kind of money to breeze through a PhD program, and be a socialite who sponsors the arts, and travel like she does. It just... I don't know people like that. People in the field don't wear designer clothes and aren't trailed by a security detail. So she's involved somehow, and I think she might be involved in art smuggling." She frowned and hesitated. "In fact, I hate to say this, but I think she might've gotten me involved in white-washing the whole thing."

"How so?" Walt was relaxed into a big easy chair and the ice was all melted in his drink, rendering its color as pale as a winter sunrise.

"She got some affidavits from the local clergy that supposedly say she has their artifact in safekeeping so that some museum doesn't appropriate it. That's been an issue in the past."

"I know." He waved at her to continue.

"She had me take photos of all the documentation, and the artifacts, and everything. In case her file box got stolen or destroyed. Or confiscated, I guess."

"What did the affidavits say?"

She sipper her whiskey again and realized she was the only one drinking. She set it down on a side table, placed her hands on her knees, and shook her head. "I don't know. It was in Serbian, and I'd have to sit over it for a while to figure it out. The Cyrillic they use is different enough from Russian, and I don't really speak the language. I could infer things, but it's not the same."

"No, it is not." Walt nodded. "So what else pushed your buttons about Peter Christoff?"

She felt the heat rise up her face again, but didn't reach for the whiskey again. "He and his wife have an open relationship."

He nodded, nonplussed. "So you slept with him. Or with her."

"No!" She felt like a teenager who got caught necking behind her parent's garage. "No, we just, we just kissed. And then he got a phone call, and had to go. In the middle of the night!" Her sense of propriety warred with her indignity at being stood up like that, and if Walt's twitch in the corner of his mouth meant anything, it showed.

"You are laughing at me, Walt. Go ahead, I was a fool. There were more important things to do than, you know." Her fingers were intertwined on top of her knees as she leaned forward, wishing she had something to do with her hands. "But I followed him 'cause I was pissed that he left just like that. And, well. Then I saw the Stingers. Nobody should be dealing Stingers out of the back of a car in the middle of nowhere like that. In the middle of a war zone."

"Why not?" Walter asked. "They have all kinds of weapons. The Soviets have pretty good infrared guided rockets, too."

"I told you about my brother Tony, right?"

"No." He leaned forward, indicating interest."

"He was a Ranger."

"Was?" He frowned.

"He got hurt bad in Mogadishu and got a medical discharge. And as you're probably aware, the whole city was armed to the teeth with various weapons. What you might not be aware of is that some of the Somalis used

American-made weapons. Tony saw the guy who shot him – he'd been a gunner on a Humvee and had it not been the armor-piercing ammo that some enterprising fuckhole lifted off the base and sold to the locals, the armor might not have failed, and Tony might still have a usable left arm." She seethed, eyes narrowed and nostrils flared, with her tight jaw pointed straight at Walt in his easy chair.

"You picked up a great deal from your brother," Walt remarked, and took a healthy sip of his drink. "Including language."

"Fuck language. This is serious. You just sit there and puff on your pipe and relax, while an unknown party has five Stingers. I'll have you know that Stingers have a lot better navigation system than the rockets the Soviets originated. And they go further. You can down an airliner with one of those, as long as you can see its outline, and that's often. In fact, I'd bet you that Peter Christoff uses the same people to smuggle goods as his wife does."

"You think? How would that work?"

"You tell me. You're the cultural attaché."

He sighed. "Gina. You give me valuable insight, and I am curious to see where this will lead us."

"Us? I did all I could."

"Did you? All you could?"

She didn't answer. Smoke hung heavy in the air. She shifted, and a piece of heavy paper crackled in the pocket of her jeans.

The decision came upon her suddenly and Gina stood up and extricated the worn envelope. "I have been sort of hesitating to hand this over," she said. "I'm not sure why, really. Maybe because I stole it, and I have never stolen anything before. Or because my first effort at taking a picture of it failed, and now it feels like a trophy of sorts."

She took several steps and stopped before Walt's easy chair. "Here you go. I can't read it anyway."

He put the pipe in the ash tray next to his drink, and accepted her offering. "But I can," he said with a Cheshire Cat smile.

She watched him pull out the heavy stock and unfold it again. He hummed as he let his thumb run over the embossed crest in the letterhead. "The letterhead paper seems genuine." He put it up against a light bulb and peered at it for some time before he just set the letter on the table. He read it in silence. When he looked up, his expression was clouded.

"What's wrong?"

"This letter doesn't say what your friend Peter thought it would say."

"What does it say?"

Walt leaned back and looked at her. His expression was speculative. "I am sorry, dear Gina, but you don't have the need to know."

She stood like a pillar of salt. It was right there in front of them, black on white. Little squiggly characters of the Cyrillic alphabet wavered on the creamy stock in the warm and indirect light of the reading room, making the letter seem antique, imbuing it with importance.

"Okay," she said after some time passed, and receded back to her chair. "I understand you can't tell me certain things. But is there anything you *can* tell me? Remember, I'll be moving in the region for another two years, if I can secure grant funding. If there is anything you'd like me to be aware of, please let me know."

She leaned back and picked up her unfinished drink again. She pretended to take a casual sip, like knowledge didn't matter. She was just an art student, true, but this world of finding things intrigued her adventurous streak, beckoned to her with its shadows rich in hidden meanings. She waited.

Walt seemed to have been observing her under his heavy eyelids. When he broke the silence, it was in a conversational tone, as though what he was saying didn't really matter. As thought the information he relayed to her did not mean potential life or death, if not for her, then for others who stumbled in blind.

"That line you said before, Gina. Your idea that art smuggling and gun running happens using the same, or at least similar, routes. How interesting. It's not a new idea, but it's not something we can pay more attention to. Of course, my hands are tied. There is nothing I can do from this office." He sighed and picked up his pipe again. "Of course, if I knew at least one of Peter Christoff's associates…"

"Then what?" Gina said when the silence became too heavy.

"Then I could find someone to keep an eye on that person."

"And what kind of information would you be looking for? Speaking just theoretically, of course." Gina was glad she'd retreated back to her chair. The air was cleaner a few feet away from Walt, but she also felt in a better possession of her faculties. More in control. Less apt to burst out random facts.

Control was good.

Control was, in fact, paramount.

"It would be interesting to see what kind of art passes through his customer's hands. And what other artifacts. And where it goes. Theoretically speaking."

Gina bit her lip. She had never been to Cyprus, and Cyprus was in the south and away from the snow.

It was tempting.

She had an introduction to Peter's fence, and she had her own interests when it came to finding the original sites of the stolen artifacts. This could be a win-win situation. Except she couldn't afford it.

"Maybe in the spring," she said, and the regret in her voice was genuine. "I have to get back to Ravenna, and I have to write another grant proposal. Grad school's expensive. Travel's expensive. Writing proposals takes as much time as gathering data and writing papers. It's like having a second job."

"Is that so." Walt chewed on his pipe. The fire went out, but he didn't bother relighting it. "There might be a scholarship out there for you."

"I think I applied for everything already."

"I don't think you did. I think you could get a particular scholarship, which would fund your studies and your travel to Cyprus. Theoretically speaking."

She smiled. "Of course, you realize I don't speak Cypriot."

"The official languages are Turkish and Greek, although they've been using English in the courts for a year or two. Almost everyone there speaks English. Remember, it used to be a British colony not so long ago." He gave her a searching look. "You'd be on your own. No risks. No balconies, no trellises, no getting personal. Just do your art stuff and keep your eyes open."

"And what, send you a report?" She grinned, knowing the answer.

"I dislike paperwork. However, I do like Ravenna. I'll meet you there, you take me out for good Italian food, show me a museum."

"Okay."

"Okay."

They didn't shake hands. She was on her own, and there was that old thrill of adventure in the air. She had a secret, and that, too, thrilled her. The only thing that galled her was not knowing what was in that letter.

CHAPTER 17

PETER DIALED the familiar number. It rang and rang, and just before he thought the answering machine would pick up, a woman's voice answered.

"Hello?" She sounded younger than her years, soft and deep. Peter smiled despite himself.

"Aunt Yelena, it's me."

"Ah!" She exclaimed without saying his name. She was well used to their routine. "Do you want to talk to your uncle?"

"Just briefly. In private, please." They both knew what that meant.

"Do you have a number?"

"Yes." Peter read off a series of digits, said good-bye, and hung up. Then he fought his way out of the too-small telephone booth and walked two blocks up and one block over. Another telephone booth stood by the edge of a concrete sidewalk, yellow and noticeable in the snowy twilight. It was four o'clock in the afternoon and Vienna was almost dark. Not too cold, though, despite the snowfall. Picturesque as it was, snow never lasted long in these parts. He was glad for the temperate climate. Last thing they needed right now was a snow emergency.

Peter paced back and forth for a good half hour, glancing at his watch every so often, trying to visualize what must have been going on half the world away. They had seven o'clock in the morning in California, but back in the old days, Uncle Ilya would have been up for an hour already. Now Peter was not so sure. Maybe he should have waited till later. The thought of the old man weakened by chemotherapy tugged at his heart. Uncle Ilya had always been his staunchest supporter.

Oleg and Alexi didn't bear this sort of favoritism well. They were the real sons, after all, and Peter was only a nephew. Oleg's theory was that Ilya was trying to make up for having executed Peter's father when Peter was only five. This fact was never shoved into the dim and convenient past. Uncle Ilya was the patriarch, the protector, the role model. He was also the one who killed when he deemed it necessary.

Peter had never felt the need to forgive him. His father's death was a fact of life, just like Ilya's death would be. Peter wouldn't kill Uncle Ilya the way he used to imagine he would during his rebellious teens, and he no longer felt the guilt he felt for not needing to kill him as an adult. Now he only stood guard and watched the old man, wondering whether he'd die.

He missed him.

He wished Uncle Ilya had been able to come along, if only in an advisory capacity. Things weren't going as planned and somehow, somewhere, things had gone terribly wrong.

A snowflake landed on his nose and melted. By now, the California sunshine would bask Los Angeles in its glow. The weather would be just right for shorts and a T-shirt, with a long-sleeve linen shirt over it to cover the shoulder holster on his quick morning run before the smog hit. Aunt Yelena probably had Uncle Ilya dressed by now, and they were driving to a pay phone far enough from the house, but not too far. Peter wondered how secure their connection really was, how anonymous.

Yet he needed counsel. He would have sent a telegram, had the matter been less sensitive.

If Aunt Yelena did the driving these days, they would take more than the usual thirty minutes. The memory of her loathing of traffic made him smile.

The telephone in the booth rang, vibrating the glass and steel structure. The snowflakes fell as though in slow motion.

Peter fought to get to it on time. Right away. Immediately. The nighttime air thickened into molasses and by the time he lifted the receiver, he half gasped for air.

"Yeah." That's all Peter said.

"Where are you?" Uncle Ilya's voice was unmistakable, accented, and sounded like a shadow of its former self.

"Vienna."

"Everybody okay, son?"

Peter smiled. Uncle Ilya must have been either pleased or concerned if he called him 'son.'

"Yes and no." He described their trip in efficient statements that spoke of years of giving similar reports. He had loathed these missions and these reports in the past - but today was different. Depending on Uncle Ilya's condition, this might be the last report they shared.

Since his teens, Peter had wanted to be on his own, separate from the family business, away from all that was dysfunctional and broken in their tight-knit little clan. Yet his chest constricted at the thought that all this was grinding to an end.

"Well done, Peter." The old man wheezed through his thoughtful silence. Expensive seconds of international connection ticked by. "You did what you were supposed to do."

"But I didn't," Peter insisted. "I was supposed to deliver the payload to a Serbian buyer, and the guys were Bosnians! I could tell. They were armed. They would have taken it even if we hadn't agreed to the transaction."

"That's right," Uncle Ilya said, and coughed as he tried to laugh. "Peter, things are not always what they seem. You got the money?"

"Sure I got the money, but Uncle Ilya, that can't be right! It's not just about the money anymore. It's... you know what can happen with those things." Peter knew better than naming the Stingers over a connection that they only hoped was anonymous and safely lost in the din of international call traffic.

"I do know, Peter. You're a good boy. You were always a good boy, and you always tried to do the right thing." Ilya wheezed for a while, resting up. "Listen, I wish I had told you sooner. I wish we could talk about this in person. But you did the right thing this time, too."

Peter weighed the implications of the old man's words. "But... how come?"

"Hit them in the stupid, son. Just hit them in the stupid!"

145

"That's always your favorite line, but it's not obvious what you mean by it." Peter didn't voice his cold fear that they would not have this conversation in person. He wondered how big a price the old man had paid to leave his sickbed, but his concern was overshadowed by his need for vital information. "Just tell me."

"You sold them a bunch of tattle-tales. Hit 'em in the stupid."

"Okay." Peter was thinking hard. Tattle-tales. Had the merchandise been electronic equipment, or an antique, it would have been easy to implant a microphone. But how could one bug a missile? He thought hard. "How?"

"Consult a horoscope." Ilya chucked, then coughed.

Aunt Yelena came on the line. "Peter dear, we do need to turn in now. Thank you for calling. Come home soon?"

"As soon as I can," Peter promised.

"Good. Oh, wait up." There was a brief silence. "Uncle says, don't forget to bring that letter. That will show who tried to run you off the road up in the mountains."

"Oh…" Peter swallowed an uncomfortable lump in his throat.

"You do have the letter, dear, don't you?" Yelena wasn't one to miss the beat.

"No… I am afraid I do not. I couldn't find it anywhere."

"Who was near it?" Her voice got older all of a sudden, and as sharp as a knife.

"Just me and Vera. It was in my coat pocket… and my coat… oh."

"Think, Peter!"

"It's impossible. But one of the people we smuggled out of Serbia could have picked it up. Zhenia came recommended by Uncle Ilya's contact, and he's the one with the clavicle fracture. He was in a lot of pain." But he had a sling, Peter thought, and that sling could have concealed the letter easily.

"And the other person?" She asked.

"A student we picked up. She got stuck behind the lines and needed to get out. An American."

"Young and pretty, I imagine. Peter, your predilections will bring you nothing but trouble. She's the one who took it, no doubt."

"She didn't speak Serbian!"

146

"That you know of." Yelena's voice betrayed no small amount of anger. "And what of Vera?"

"Vera liked her. The girl helped her catalogue some artifacts Vera was collecting." Peter was on full defensive by now. The old woman saw more than he figured she ever would.

"And did the girl like you?" She asked, and her voice softened somewhat.

"Not nearly enough," he said with a bitter laugh. "She preferred the company of my wife."

"Ah, a good girl, then," Yelena said with audible relief.

"Yes. I got her set up with my contact so she could continue working in her field."

There was silence for a while, not just the two-second delay between words and phrases, but a deep, transoceanic hum. Yelena was the one to break it.

"Peter, you're such an idiot! You had no way to know if she was trustworthy! Now she can connect you to them, and..." Yelena paused, and Peter heard an echo of Uncle Ilya's sharp words. "Get home immediately. We have some talking to do before your Uncle passes on. God knows, nobody is perfect. I just wish you knew when to keep your trousers on!"

CHAPTER 18

Gina arrived in Ravenna to the worried exclamations of her landlady, and to the relieved fluttering of her academic advisor. Her room had been dusted regularly, and was aired out, but as far as she could tell, Signora Conti hadn't touched a thing. It occurred to Gina that she had never before looked for signs of tampering.

Her adventures were messing with her mind.

She settled in, wrote a sizeable report that referred to her academic subject matter alone, and managed to secure several hours of darkroom time to develop the numerous rolls of film from the trip. It was cheaper to do her own instead of sending it out, and it was certainly faster. This way, she could include photo prints to assuage her advisor and showcase the nature of her work in her future grant applications.

The utter, deep-space darkness of the darkroom accentuated her other senses. The pads of her fingertips softened, alert to the shapes and textures in her hands as she wound her film from the roll onto a plastic spool by touch alone. Winding film was almost hypnotic. Her mind wandered to Walt. She wondered if he'd come through with her scholarship. That way, she could spend less time over grant applications.

Roll after roll and spool after spool, she immersed the film in the developer and pushed the button of the preset alarm clock. Her sense of smell intensified in the darkness and the chemicals filled the enclosed space with a familiar, vaguely acidic odor, much like a chemistry lab back in high school. The alarm clock ticked away, and she knew parts of it were moving in the dark where she couldn't see them.

Half an hour.

Normally it would have felt like forever, but she had much to think about.

Gina pulled a stick of mint gum out of her pocket, and almost pulled a piece out before she remembered that, oh yeah, she was working with chemicals and eating was ill advised. She did catch a whiff of mint, though, and that reminded her of the time she sat on her bed in that old little hotel in the mountains and chewed stick after a stick, making a makeshift glue to conceal the means of her entry into Peter and Vera's room.

She smiled in the dark, still finding it hard to believe that she'd actually done all that, and had seen all that, and that she'd reported it all to Walt at the embassy in Vienna.

She wondered whether "cultural attaché" actually meant a "CIA agent." An operative. A spook. She had been tempted to ask, but she knew they would never tell her the truth. Too bad. She kind of liked Walt and his crazy-uncle mannerisms.

She also disliked the clothes-horse and his dripping condescension. The one with no need to know. She smiled again.

What an asshole.

THE SEMESTER was officially over and Gina's work was all handed in, shiny photo prints and paper reports printed on an old daisy-wheel printer. She sauntered out of the department building and onto the pavement that consisted of an ancient and elaborate mosaic. She barely kept herself from whistling and felt the pull of a smile on her face.

She ducked into a bistro for a quick pasta lunch, escaped the unwanted attentions of the proprietor in good cheer, and headed off to the nearby university library. The baroque building was vast and lit like a cathedral to all human knowledge, and she walked through her favorite areas before she moved from the card catalogue to the reference section.

Ten minutes later, she was sitting on one of the old, carved-wood chairs upstairs with their quaint leather and horsehair upholstery. The study hall was deserted.

Before her sat an Italian-Serbian, Serbian-Italian dictionary, a notebook, and the largest print of a photograph of that letter of passage

149

that she could make and still get crisp outlines. Her official work as an art student might be over for the next two weeks – but her unofficial job as a pair of curious eyes and ears had only begun.

Going to Cyprus might prove dangerous - unless she learned what was in that letter of passage.

HOURS PASSED. Gina stretched up and leaned back to crack her spine against her chair. The leaded windows darkened with the oncoming evening, and the glowing, yellow reading lights at the library desks lent warmth to the cavernous space. She felt like her tabletop was a floating island in a vast sea, bobbing along in the dusk, and then it came to her that it was all just an artifact of eye strain, and she put her pencil down.

The letter was translated, but that didn't mean she understood exactly what it said. It introduced Peter Christoff and his cavalcade of three vehicles. It informed the reader that he was an ally of the Serbian government. It granted him free passage in and out of the territory without fee or hindrance. Illegible signature and a smeared stamp marked the end.

But there was that last line under it. She tried to figure out what it meant, especially since it was hand-written in ballpoint pen. All numbers and letters of the Serbian alphabet.

A code.

The dictionary was recent. It took her some time to figure out what certain Cyrillic letters sounded like in Serbian, and once she was able to pronounce the words, she was able to draw a parallel between them and their Russian equivalents in roughly two-thirds of all cases. She checked them using the dictionary just to be sure, and found eight errors. For the last one third, she looked up every word and made the best of it she could.

No dictionary in the world would tell her what that hand-written line of code meant.

Gina thought back. The embassy, old Walt and the warm scent of his pipe tobacco. The peaty bite of her first-ever whiskey.

Walt had seen the letter, and he did betray a certain air of unease. There was nothing in this letter that should've caused that.

Nothing.

Except for that cipher on the bottom.

THE SEQUENCE of letters and numbers stayed firmly etched in her mind as she packed for Cyprus, knowing the money for her stay and passage sat heavy in the security pocket of her jacket. Her camera was clean, she had fresh film, her duffel was packed with clean clothes. She was looking forward to the balmy weather of the Mediterranean, the briny sea breeze, the sunrise and the sunset.

Curiosity spurred her on to make the night train to Messina and, after bumming around Messina for the day, she boarded the next boat to Cyprus. She sat on the upper deck, shielded from the wind by a plexiglass screen as she sipped a glass of cheap wine. Her things were in a little cabin she shared with a small, elderly Greek woman that read books and drank Ouzo in the common room near the prow. Gina grinned at her good luck. She had never been on a sea voyage before, and the train and the ferry were both cheaper than flying. Her backpack was well stocked with academic reading materials, but those could wait for later. First she would enjoy the sunset, sip some wine, and relish her three and a half days at sea. And best of all, she would most decidedly not think about that last sentence from the letter of passage.

CHAPTER 19

ZENO LIPERTIS ran an art dealership and a storage warehouse less than two kilometers from the Limassol harbor, but Gina was still right by the water's edge of Cyprus' largest port city.

Fresh ocean breeze whispered of diesel and fish. The hum of engines and the sonorous blow of horns from afar cut through the gentle splashing of the waves against the dock.

Gina squinted against the brutal glare of the sun. The paper she held had the address and an inadequate sketch of a map, which she'd copied from a large map at the university library. She knew where she was right now, but she hadn't bothered to draw in the side streets, and that had been a mistake.

She shoved the sketch into the pocket of her too-warm jacket, hoisted her backpack and her duffle bag, and walked along the water, keeping the steep concrete drop-off to her left and massive warehouses to her right. The trip on the modest boat had been uneventful, the weather fabulous, and she was a bit disappointed not to have gotten seasick along with several other passengers because she'd been reading about seasickness in books and had a hard time imagining it.

Cyprus was firm under her feet.

She grinned.

A sense of elation buoyed her, because she'd never been here before. New adventure awaited, and she had absolutely no idea what in the world was going to happen next. She'd visit Peter's fence, of course, and she'd see if he'd let her look at his wares. He might even shed some light at the convoluted paths smugglers used – not that she'd ever accuse him – and that information would be useful to Walter, the friendly cultural attaché in Vienna.

She'd report stray bits of information, Walter would arrange for a scholarship. What wasn't to like?

The docks went on for a few more blocks until streets opened to her right. She was delighted to see several stores. Gina knew her lack of knowledge of both Greek and Turkish would be a hindrance, and even though Arabic was one of the minority languages on the island, her fluency was nowhere near adequate for business purposes. That's why she almost squealed in glee at multi-lingual store and road signs. She knew the road signs would show English, but that's where the English ended.

Store signs were just as important. Every store, without fail, had the sign and their specials translated into Russian.

This Russian connection was an unexpected boon, and after days of eavesdropping on Peter and his crew, she picked up the meaning of the signs with ease.

She stopped by an open door. The unmistakable music of spoken Russian drifted out, and she felt a sense of satisfaction when she understood most of it.

Suddenly a bit shy, Gina took a few steps away from the door and leaned against the stucco wall. The little travelogue she read on board ship had informed her that Cyprus had been in contact with Russia as far as nine hundred years ago. She skimmed over some stuff regarding orthodox churches and pilgrimage routes. The Soviet Union had supported Cyprus since 1960 or so. In fact, despite its civil war between the Greek and the Turkish populations, the Soviets had an embassy in Nicosia, and the Greek Cypriots had an embassy in Moscow.

From what she'd read, the Russians were involved in all kinds of things even now. The Iron Curtain fell two years prior. That alone should have called an end to the Cold War, but the shifting winds of power stirred up other kinds of trouble. The Balkans, the Middle East, and the Soviet withdrawal from Afghanistan were on her mind as she contemplated territories that were once proxy-war playgrounds.

Now they were in a state of upheaval – and power abhors a vacuum.

Gina looked up and down the street at the Russian signage. The USSR would either disintegrate, or change. What would become of Cyprus then? Would the old conflict flare up again, or would the Russians maintain enough of a presence to keep things under their obvious control?

The Mediterranean sun was almost blinding as it reflected off the whitewashed buildings across the street, and off the placid water of the harbor she could see down an alley.

She needed sunglasses.

Something to eat and drink wouldn't hurt either, and she needed a real map.

Hell, she needed a plan. Taking a pleasant boat ride would have normally lulled her into a vacation mindset, yet she was keenly aware that this was no time to relax. Gina thought back to Serbia, to Hungary, and to their haphazard flight toward Vienna. No matter what Peter and Vera Christoff were doing right now, or what Zhenia was doing or how his arm was healing, she needed to anchor her mind in the present and take in her surroundings.

Alert, aware, and observant.

The photograph of the letter was safely tucked in her backpack, but the last line, the hand-written line of letters and numbers, bothered her.

Why include this on an official letter?

Anyone could've added that – anyone with access to state correspondence between the time the letter had been signed in Belgrade, and the moment it was either mailed or placed directly into Peter Christoff's hands.

Probably the latter.

The Cyrillic of the Serbian letter made her think of the Cyrillic imprint on the crates of weapons back in Zabljak.

She was here to meet a man and talk about antiques. She was here to investigate smuggling routes for stolen artifacts. And, while she was at it, she hoped to snoop around a bit. If Zeno's warehouse was big enough, surely it wasn't beyond the pale to get lost in it with her camera in her backpack.

She might even run into a bulky shipment of something other than smuggled pottery.

Spurred by the thought, Gina left the lee of the doorway and started walking.

A LEISURELY half-hour stroll brought her to a loose tangle of streets. Warehouses and maintenance businesses began to give way to residential homes with their flat roofs and palm-tree gardens. A general store on the corner looked like it might have what she needed.

Gina ducked in. She stopped, letting her eyes adjust to the dim interior. A fan spun overhead in lazy circles and a soccer match ran on a small television behind the counter. A middle-aged woman with bottle-blond hair and heavy make-up looked her up and down.

"Hello," Gina said.

"Khello!" The woman beamed her a smile. Her gold tooth glinted as though it was coordinated with her hoop earrings on purpose. "Khow may I khelp you?"

Her heavy Russian accent was a relief. There was another language to fall back upon if necessary. "Do you have sunglasses?" Gina asked.

"Over there."

Gina picked a pair, found an overpriced map, and chose a bottle of an orange drink off the shelf. It wasn't chilled, and after her months in the area, she knew better than asking for ice. She chose two snacks, figuring they'd be sweet and contain nuts, and headed for the counter.

"You lost?" The woman glanced up and down as she made change.

"No." She wasn't, not really. All she needed was a shady passageway so she could read the map and orient herself.

"Ah. American?" The shop keeper gave her a curious look.

"Yes. Student."

"Ah. Welcome to Cyprus. Our weather very good here."

"Yes, it is." Gina smiled. She didn't want to be remembered and therefore she didn't smile too much. Just enough not to seem rude.

"You know where to go?" The woman set her hands on the counter and leaned forward, getting a lot farther into Gina's personal space than her American sensibility dictated. It was very Middle Eastern. She thought of shrugging it off, but that might seem strange for someone who's just a student on a holiday.

Gina took a step back.

The woman smiled. "You stay with someone?"

Gina nodded. "Yes. A friend." And if she dropped a name, the shop keeper was sure to spread the news before the day was halfway over. "Thank you," she said instead, took her things, and disappeared.

TEN MINUTES later, she landed in a small square with a coffee shop that offered outdoor seating under a broad awning. Its green and white stripes filtered the merciless sun, and Gina gratefully ordered an iced tea as she pulled her map out.

The ocean was that way, and the sun was to her left, which meant she was facing... north?

She peered at the map. The harbor, the docks, the intersections. Warehouses and small villas and a quaint intersection – here – and two block later, the coffee shop.

I'm here.

And now for the address of Zeno's warehouse. The map didn't have a grid like the American maps she was used to. The street wasn't one of the big streets – she checked them one by one, going from the harbor up. North was up, and she was facing north, which was good, because it made left and right turns obvious.

She'd never had these issues in Italy or the Balkans, because she'd look at the map and the train schedule, and the train would take her to where she needed to go. Trains were cheap and easy to use. Walking in terrain wasn't too hard, because country roads connected villages with interesting architectural features. As long as she stuck to the road, she knew she'd get to her destination eventually.

The cities, though. They were the worst. Hard pavement, hills and gorges, twisty-turny streets that confused her already bad sense of direction. When she was figuring out Florence for the first time, she wasn't above turning the map so that she always proceeded in the direction of travel.

She couldn't do that now. Wandering through Limassol with an upside-down map in her hands just because she was going south instead of north would have drawn too much attention.

Damn.

The old-fashioned way, then. She pored over the map a bit longer. Zino Lippertis' antique business was in the warehouse district, but on the other side of the harbor. She should've taken a right off the boat, not left.

Now that she knew, she pulled out a small piece of paper and drew a little cheat map, marking large intersections by name. She left money for her tea and a small baksish, stowed her map in the backpack, and left.

SUN BEHIND me is east.

Gina zigged and zagged through the ancient streets, enjoying both the sun-drenched cityscape and the vibrant, blooming flowers that climbed out of their pots and swayed in the stiff ocean breeze. Part of her journey took her along the busy downtown full of cars and motorcycles, past expensive stores and full restaurants.

The tourists were in for the winter. That was good – it made it easier to get lost in the crowd.

A hotel beckoned, with its rich portico and balconies that ran from room to room, trailing red flowers from window boxes. So cheerful, red against white. And she'd need a place to stay.

On a lark, Gina walked in to explore her options. The place was expensive for the locals, but the dollar exchange rate made it affordable. She paid for a room for one night, cash, and walked two flights of stairs to drop her duffle bag in the small room.

A brief inspection confirmed a small, private bathroom with a Western-type toilet. Good – she didn't particularly feel like dealing with a Turkish hole in the floor. The two narrow beds seemed clean and the work gilding on the Venetian mirror gave the space an antique feel. The room smelled dry, like a ceramic studio. She touched the white wall, surprised to find white paint residue on her fingertips.

She smelled it.

That's where that old clay odor came from. With luck, it would be just that and not a toilet backing up in the middle of the night. Not like in that old place in Szeged, where she and Vera had been plagued by the angry toilet god all night long.

The memory of Vera, sneaking around with a loaded pistol, gave her a shiver. She was abroad and unarmed. A gun would be nice just about now, especially if she knew what to do with it. Or pepper spray. Anything – any weapon.

She'd never felt a need for a weapon before.

Interesting.

Gina changed into off-white linen trousers that had been washed into a wrinkle-free softness over the last three years, and pulled on an aqua blue shirt. That, her backpack, and her sensible leather sandals, and she almost blended into the crowds of tourists.

Gathering information.

That's what she was there to do. Not spying, or fighting, or sneaking up a trellis into someone else's room. Just plain talk, an interested look-around, maybe an interview she could reference in her thesis next year.

No weapons. Weapons would only get her in trouble down the road.

She gave the face in the mirror an innocent smile. *Better.* To all strange eyes, she was on a leisurely vacation. Once she left her room and locked it, she planned to wear that sweet, relaxed expression wherever she went.

Gina took a complimentary map on her way out. The hotel's location was clearly marked on it. She folded it, shoved it in her pocket, and marched on.

CHAPTER 20

The warehouse didn't look like any other warehouse Gina had ever seen. The three-story building rose up from a small side street in a neighborhood of local shops and residences. The facade looked new and modern, but the sandstone surrounding each window and the central doorway was old, stained with an aged patina which almost obscured the ancient tool marks and faintly carved geometric designs.

Gina stopped, lifted her sunglasses, and squinted against the glare that reflected off the upper part of the building. Her vision adjusted after a time. Comfortable in the shade of other structures, she checked the address before she peered at the old stonework again.

If the light and ambiance didn't play tricks on her, those carvings were old. Ancient, worn, possibly pre-Hellenic. Certainly too old for a three-story building that housed Tradewind Antique Galleries. Someone had done a great job copying a rare original.

She could've been inside already – should've been – yet she hesitated. A flurry of butterflies rose in her stomach.

Stagefright.

How quaint, feeling awkward just because Zeno Lipertis was Peter's contact. How silly, worrying about nothing.

She wanted this information. Didn't she?

International art smuggling routes were real.

Finding out more was important – she might even see long-lost artifacts inside. Especially if she didn't levy baseless accusations, if she showed her interest to be purely academic.

159

A gust of warm wind caressed her face. She almost felt it push her toward the entrance.

She pressed the old, cast-iron lever on the shop door. Zeno Lipertis seemed to be careful with his property, if the fresh green paint on the ancient wood was any indication. He was careful and he respected the old things, the imperfect things. If he had not, he'd have replaced the small, uneven glass panes with something modern and devoid of both bubbles and character.

A bell rang overhead. Gina stepped in, sliding her tired feet against the rough, terra-cotta tile floor. The door clicked shut behind her and she took few more steps into the crowded, narrow room. It was lined with shelves and glass-paned curio cabinets, cluttered with display counters, filled with artifacts. An ancient register sat on a wooden counter to her left, shiny with grape-and-leaf decorations that enlivened the dim space.

"Hello?" English seemed like a good bet. Gina called out and listened for an answer. "Hello!"

Her voice didn't even seem to echo through – the furniture, books, and fixtures absorbed it as though she had been surrounded by acoustic tiles.

Maybe nobody could hear her.

She hesitated, walked the length of the room, and peeked through the open doorway. There was another room, with an annex to the right and another to the left. Daylight poured through the tall windows, illuminating categories of artifacts.

A cursory glance told her Zeno Lipertis organized his finds according to their region and time period, not according to a particular type of an object. Some gallery owners liked having a painting room, a sculpture room, and so on. Here, though, the spaces were filled as though the building had been a museum, and the owner curated the artifacts as much as resold them.

Interesting.

The case to her right was full of Egyptian scarabs and seals. Gina drifted closer, hoping for a closer look, when a glance through the next doorway distracted her entirely. The space going back was huge and cavernous and filled with islands of goods. Each island consisted of several wood pallets and was stacked with crates. Different sizes, different materials. Some looked old and dusty, others had fresh paper labels and official stamps.

The warehouse.

Gina grinned. That's where Zeno Lipertis must've gone! She looked around and, not seeing anyone, she walked in. A single glance told her it was built onto the back of the handsome house, whose three stories and a stucco facade were enlivened by ancient carvings. Its structure and the way its gold-tone stucco had gleamed in the sunlight when she'd first set eyes on it half an hour ago, it reminded her of the tombs in Petra. Like in that last old Indiana Jones movie, where treasures untold continued into the recesses of the mountain.

She drew a deep breath and filled her lungs, ready to call forth in earnest. Somebody must've been here, minding the shop.

Crash.

She bit her lip and froze. Something fell, far away, and it wasn't small. Another crash – and another.

A loud crack split the air like thunder – to her left and further down. She ducked and ran.

Shitshitshitshitshit...

That crack – she'd heard it before. A gun shot.

A deep voice cursed – she didn't know in what language – and another barked three foreign words.

A scream.

Two more gun shots. One yelp of pain.

She was running on her toes now, holding the straps to keep her backpack from bouncing. She ducked, leaned against a dusty crate, and fought to keep her breath still and even. The crate's rough joinery dug into her shoulder blade and the dust she raised threatened to make her sneeze.

Now what?

She didn't even get to meet Zeno Lipertis. Someone was in here now. Something bad had just happened, and if she couldn't question Peter's contact, she could at least have a look.

While staying hidden.

The camera? No. No flash. *A dead give-away, and its whirring sound would sound like thunder.*

161

A peek, then. A look, slow and easy, in the dark. Like creeping down the trellis, like removing a glass pane from Peter's balcony door.

Those crates all around her – they could've contained weapons, statues, mummies. There was no way to tell, no time to check, and nobody to ask. She now realized how naive she'd been, thinking she could take pictures of an illicit, smuggled arsenal and pass it on to old Walt.

She would only look.

Grateful for the soft soles of her sandals, she tiptoed around the crate and peeked out.

Nothing.

She crossed the aisle and crouched behind the next bulky load.

Breathe. Just breathe.

She heard a scraping sound - like someone was dragging a thing.

Or a body.

Raspy breath and a choked-back curse carried on the still, warehouse air to her ears.

She peeked out again.

Nothing.

She repeated the process, hiding behind the next stack of crates, and the next, until she was halfway across the warehouse.

Old industrial lights spilled their yellow glow from the far-away ceiling fixtures over the central aisle. The space was dim and the shadows by the walls were inky dark.

She cursed her off-white trousers and pale blue shirt. Too visible.

A gurgle and a cough.

She froze.

Siss... siss... siss... the sound of something being dragged was back.

Gina risked a peek around the crate. Just one eye.

A man was on his hands and one knee, head drooping to the floor, blond hair falling over his face.

Siss...siss... siss...

The sound of something dragging was him, dragging his leg. His bleeding, bloody, shot-apart leg with dark stains seeping up and down his tan trousers. His white shirt was wet with sweat and plastered to his back – no undershirt, damp body hair - and she wondered whether his front would be stained with blood, too.

162

Gina thought maybe she should help him, but Zeno Lipertis probably didn't have blond hair like this wounded stranger. This was an intruder, then, and if he was, there might be more.

Armed people were probably lurking behind the loaded wooden pallets of the cavernous warehouse, melting into the shadows with their loaded guns and trained silence.

She swallowed bile at the thought.

The man lurched two more feet, gasped for air, and collapsed onto the worn and dusty floor.

Her senses heightened, she could now smell the spent gunpowder and the metallic tang of blood in the air. She saw the outlines of shadows in places previously too dark for her vision – and she knew she couldn't tell whether the shapes in the recesses of darkness were real or imagined, friend of foe.

The not knowing terrified her.

The man stopped crawling.

Seconds ticked by with infuriating slowness. She heard her watch mark the relentless passage of time just two feet away from her face.

If she heard her watch, how come she couldn't hear the others?

The man stopped gasping for air.

Thirty-two minutes later, Gina inched her way toward him. She peeked around the corner, up and down the main aisle of the warehouse.

Nobody. Just silence, broken by a claxon of an unknown ship in the harbor for endless seconds. When the sound ceased, the silence weighed heavier and darker upon her.

Gina squared her shoulders and walked toward the man.

He was still, and when she bent toward him, his shoulder was warm to her hesitant touch. She thought she should check his pulse, the way she saw it done in the movies, to see if he was alive or dead, but the heavy smear of blood he left behind told her what she needed to know.

Dead. Her first dead man.

Walt would want to know what had happened back there, but finding out required going back there and... finding out.

She thought her stomach should turn, or she should puke, or faint, or something – but her gut had settled after the initial bout of fear. Now that she had straightened up, she felt normal in that sort of creepy and detached way serial killers probably feel normal as they go about their business.

She didn't feel a thing.

The blood trail told her where to go and prepared her for what she'd see.

Another man – Caucasian, in his thirties, dead. A hole in his chest, a gun in his hand. He looked a lot like the first corpse, dressed in navy trousers instead of tan, but his shirt was a white button-down and his black leather shoes looked sturdy and practical.

Was *this* Zeno Lipertis? And if so, why was there a gun fight?

Except she expected Zeno Lipertis to be dark and swarthy, and older than Peter by at least ten years. He was supposed to be a well-established businessman.

So where was he?

She looked around. Just crates, more crates and labels, although this section was nearly dust-free. A lot newer.

She turned a corner and tripped in the dark.

She fell - someone screamed.

A hard piece of metal dug into her shoulder.

Ewww.

Sticky moisture underhand.

She stilled. An echo of the sound died down. Her throat was hoarse and her eyes stung with unshed tears of distress – that's when she realized it had been her scream that had split the sepulchral silence.

Like Petra, this shop was a tomb, complete with treasures untold and its own collection of bodies. One of those bodies was right under her.

Gina scampered to her feet, kicking something hard and metallic with her toe. Making it skitter to the side.

A gun?

His gun.

She made her way to the aisle where there was more light, shrugged her backpack off her shoulders, and rummaged through its outside pocket.

Flashlight.

It was small, just two AA batteries worth, but that was enough for now. Gina went back behind the stack of crates and shed light on the dead body.

The man was short and round. Soft to land upon – except for the metal thing stuck in his chest. That's what had jabbed her shoulder. It didn't look like anything familiar. Not a knife, not a sharpened screwdriver.

What *was* that thing? And was this Zeno Lipertis?

Older, darker, curly hair shot with silver threads.

Walt would want to know. Whatever happened here, she almost walked in on it. Hell, had it not been for getting lost and having to spend time finding herself again, she might've been on the floor with rest of the bodies right now.

Sometimes, being late wasn't a bad thing.

CHAPTER 21

Uncle Ralph from Hoboken wasn't just a crazy old man who stilled hooch on the roof of his apartment building. He was a retired police detective, and his crime scene stories had always stirred a dark current of forbidden adventure in Gina's soul.

Photos. Fingerprints. Evidence bags.

She knew not to disturb a crime scene – but those were American rules, applicable to American crime scenes where she knew the police was mostly good.

Mostly.

Her uncle didn't pull punches when he railed against graft and corruption.

She didn't know the rules of engagement in Cyprus. She didn't know whether the police was a neutral force sworn to serve and protect. They sure weren't like that in the Balkans.

No matter who the local police reported to or who lined their pockets, Gina knew that once they entered this gory tableau, she'd be cut off from any information at best, and held as a suspect at worst.

That detached sense of calm washed over her again. As though she was a foot outside her own body, merely observing her own actions. As though this wasn't real, wasn't happening right now, as though these dead bodies were just dressed-up Hollywood actors covered in fake blood.

Time slowed to a crawl as she ripped her camera out of her bag, slammed a fresh flash battery into its tiny compartment, and took a light meter reading.

Faces first. One man at a time.

The whirr-and-click of her camera filled the silence as she took her photos, one with flash and one without for each image.

Faces. Wounds. Whole bodies. New angles. Weapons.

All this was evidence. The location itself was evidence, even though she didn't know of what. Motive, maybe. Whether they were in this part of the warehouse by accident or by design, those crates and their labels just might shed a thin beam of light on Lipertis' death, and on the identity of his attackers.

She finished a roll, put it away, and inserted another. And another.

She rushed. Three rolls of film in twenty minutes. She paused just long enough to focus, bracing her elbow against nearby crates or against her knee as she crouched on the ground, avoiding the blood smears.

Fingerprints.

Uncle Ralph always made a big to-do over those, and so did all the police shows. Walt at the embassy would probably appreciate them as well and should get his money's worth.

Gina stowed her camera away and pulled out her sketchbook. She ripped out three sheets of clean paper right from the middle.

Her detachment wavered when she approached the body with its shot-up leg.

Her first death.

His hands were smudged with the dust off the warehouse floor, nails broken, torn.

Yet that trail of blood, darkening with time – still slick. Not like red ink anymore, no – more paint-like, its surface threatening to set like top of dark cherry pudding.

She'd never eat dark cherry pudding again.

Gina swallowed. Her gorge rose at what she was about to do. Echoes of the sweet and sour snack and tea gone wrong struggled to leave her body.

She swallowed again. *Just paint.*

An errant thought of blood types flitted in the back of her mind. It might be yet another form of evidence. Someday people would use DNA at crime scenes.

Maybe. But probably not.

167

Gina quartered another piece of paper and dipped its edge in the tacky, darkening pool of blood beside the dead man's leg. With meticulous care, she smeared the lightest layer onto his right hand, and pressed a clean sheet of drawing paper against it. It took her three tries.

There. Fingerprints.

One down and five more hands to go.

By the time she came to the oldest man, the one she'd landed on, she felt the passage of time like a nervous tic under her skin. This man – he had been shot at, but not shot dead. His death had come from something else. Something foreign, metallic, and hard.

Her shoulder ached in reminiscence.

She bent over, felt for the object, and gave it a tug. One, then another. Pulling a blade out of a dead man's body was surprisingly difficult, as though the flesh had closed around it and sucked its way onto it, not wanting to let it go.

She braced her foot against his bicep and wiggled it back and forth.

A blade came out – sharp and pointy. A blade without a handle.

How curious.

She wiped the gore on the dead man's trousers and sacrificed her tourist map as wrapping paper, securing the sharp-looking blade between her camera case and her sketchbook.

THE SOUND of voices made her freeze. With quiet care she tiptoed back between the crates, hiding in the shadows that she now believed to be devoid of gunmen and nighttime terrors.

Closer, then closer still.

She ghosted from crate to crate, hiding, listening. Retracing the steps that had taken her to a scene of horror and violence and gore. The double door connecting the warehouse to the front building beckoned as dust motes danced in the light filtering through the old windows and reflected off white walls, glass display cases and dark, polished furniture.

"Where the devil is he?" A man's voice drifted through the varied space, bouncing and scattering. The speaker sounded British and irritated.

"We're fifteen minutes early," a woman replied. A thud of something followed her statement. Exclamations, muttered curses, an attempt at stifled giggles and setting things to rights.

There had been a staircase in the back of the house. Gina used the commotion to tiptoe through a room of priceless bric-a brac and slowly took the steps by twos, relieved that the stairs were made of stone and wouldn't creak.

She balanced on her toes, smudged and bloody hands stuck out for balance but not daring to touch the whitewashed wall or the wrought iron banister.

"He might've stepped out for a cup of coffee," the other man said, and Gina heard the swishing of paper as though pages were being turned. "Irresponsible, that. Not even locking up! This is our investment we're talking about. Just about any bloke could waltz right in and steal the goods from under our noses!"

"Oh shut up." The woman's voice was almost drowned out by the scrape of something – a chair? Wood screeched against wood. "I'll just sit and wait."

Investment. Now that was a big word. It didn't occur to Gina that a businessman as well established as Lipertis would need investors at all. She wondered what they were into. Art? Stolen or legit? Or weapons?

She might be able to find out – as soon as she got all this blood and grime off her hands.

THE SECOND story of the house had an apartment with its own door, and that door was locked. More the pity, too, because Gina needed access to running water. She eyed the lock. It was modern and past her skill level. She'd spend too much time picking it and make noise while coaxing the tumblers to align. The people downstairs would come up and find her, bloody-handed, breaking in.

Not good.

The staircase led up, though, and she took her chances and followed it. If the party below was fifteen minutes early, she had at least that long, probably longer, before one of them got curious and decided to investigate the warehouse.

Air became rare as urgency washed over her. She needed to get out – and she couldn't just walk out past all those people, those investors, downstairs. The hard stone steps felt cool even through her sandals.

Another step, then two. Pause, listen.

A fresh breeze washed over her, carrying the scent of roast meat and a whisper of the salty ocean nearby.

Gina's stomach growled so loud she feared it would echo up and down the house. The breeze, though – there must've been a window open.

She tiptoed all the way upstairs as fast as she could and remain silent. A locked apartment door faced her, again. Same white-painted wood, same high-quality lock. Yet there was a woven straw mat with a pair of men's house slippers and a pair of hiking boots next to the door.

Lipertis must've been living up here, not on the level below.

The breeze came from the open balcony door to her right. Cyprus was known for its strong wind, and the white-painted door glazed in antique bubble glass was propped ajar using two stoneware flower pots full of mature, blooming geraniums. The sunshine outside, their vibrant red blossoms and verdant foliage and the cry of the seagulls far away was at odds with Gina's sense of urgency.

Dead bodies. Gun shots. Knives. Fingerprints.

She peeked outside. The balcony spanned the width of the building and, with its masonry and stucco waist-high wall, must've been invisible from the street. The floor was tile, modern, yet arranged in a careful mosaic pattern that belied the interests of its owner. She glanced at the small, wooden table and its closed umbrella, two chairs, and a deck lounge.

How did the umbrella ever stand up to the wind?

The terra cotta tile roof gleamed orange and brilliant in the sun. She touched it. The tiles were hot, but not unbearably so. It wasn't so bad she couldn't climb she shallow slope to the open skylight only ten feet away.

"No heroics, no adventures, no trellises."

Old Walt's words echoed in her mind. She knew she'd crossed that boundary a long time ago. Not intentionally, perhaps, but here she was, on a balcony, covered in the blood of strangers and in possession of damning evidence.

"Oh, heck." Her whispered words felt alien. It was the first thing she'd said since that scream, down in the warehouse, when she fell onto the dead body of Zeno Lipertis. The man who had lived in this apartment, the one who'd broken her fall, would do her one final service.

He'd let her use his bathroom.

CHAPTER 22

Gina looked around but didn't see inconvenient natives lurk in the windows. She brought the chair to the gutter and tested it, making sure the thin copper wouldn't give way under her weight.

It didn't, and neither did the tile.

She climbed fast. The less contact with the roof, the better. The tile that felt pleasantly warm just minutes ago was a relentless, constant heat source. Gina's hands ached, red and scuffed. If she didn't hurry, she'd end up with blisters.

A slip.

Her knee touched the fired clay. She grabbed the skylight frame and bit back a harsh yelp.

Almost there.

She opened the window wider and slithered in, legs first, belly seared through the thin fabric of her shirt.

Hang.

Fall.

Her landing on the bed was fortunate, both silent and gentle even though she gasped for breath from the shock of it.

Pause. Freeze.

The small apartment was hot and stifling compared to the warehouse downstairs, but it was silent. She rolled off the bed, a large one by European standard, but made with the same square pillows and a thin, unstructured comforter encased in a white duvet she'd seen just about everywhere in the region. The whitewash of the walls was offset by dark, polished furniture and the red and blue of a rich Turkish carpet.

She spun toward the art on the walls. Icons, paintings, reliefs.

Gina gaped. So this is what happened to the lost works, the prime treasures she remembered seeing in books and academic literature. Old photographs didn't do them justice. It seemed that the shop owner didn't walk on the side of the angels – but neither did Peter.

She had to photograph these. She had to.

Clean-up first.

The small, two-rooms-and-kitchen apartment had a surprisingly large bathroom. A modern shower stall and a soaking tub, a sink, a rack full of plush towels with woven brown, tan, and aqua designs. Egyptian, probably.

The mirror over the sink was tiny, but the full-length one that was mounted on the back of the bathroom door made up for it.

Gina gasped at her own reflection.

Dust, grime, and blood. Head to toe.

Slowly, she slithered out of her backpack and kicked off her shoes. Clean-up was her first priority. She wondered how loud would the shower be, all the way upstairs, but dismissed the idea as risky. Running water through pipes might be heard all the way downstairs, and seconds were ticking by.

She stripped out of everything, grabbed a dark brown washcloth, and wet it in a conservative trickle of warm water.

In the end, cleaning up took half an hour. Bit by bit, soap then water, body part by body part.

She slipped her underwear back on and reentered the bedroom. Surely there'd be something she could wear. The man whose body broke her fall was at least twice her size, so she'd have to improvise.

None of the pants or shorts would fit. She found a stretch-fabric T-shirt, black, the sporty kind. It hung loose on her. She tucked its hem into her underwear.

She found a skimpy, European-style swimsuit. It was blue, and the pouch up front looked ridiculous on her, but her butt filled it reasonably well and wearing a bathing suit didn't make her feel as naked as if she only had her dirty undies.

And now to cover it up.

She scanned the open wardrobe. Suits, ties, shirts, belts. None of that would do. If he only had one of those wide printed scarves, she'd wear it like a wrap-around skirt.

Except he didn't.

She closed the wardrobe and the already-examined drawers, making just soft clicks, aware that the people downstairs might well be calling the police right now. Or, worse, coming upstairs with a set of keys.

A skirt, a length of fabric that wasn't a towel. Anything.

Gina opened the door to the kitchen. Her eyes fell upon the small, square table.

An embroidered tablecloth. Blue and white. Perfect.

She'd have to move the stack of mail off first, and the potted plant, but...

Air left her lungs as she choked back a scream. She crashed backward, away from the startling softness and warmth that assaulted her bare legs.

"Mrrrow."

She looked down. A grey cat with black-pointed ears and tail rubbed against her legs again, and she bent over and petted her. "Shhh."

She took the tablecloth, shut the kitchen door, and ran to the bathroom. Quick –arrange the new wrap-around skirt, Lipertis' longest belt wound twice around her. She rolled up her old, blood-stained clothes into a tidy packet and stashed it underneath the camera in her bag.

The camera.

No. There was no time to take photos of all the artwork in this place. Not this time around.

Gina was relieved to find the door unlocked from within. She pulled it almost shut, afraid the click would be deafening on the silent staircase.

How stupid was it that she worried about the cat?

When she made it down to the first floor apartment door, she heard the voices again.

"Bloody hell. Now we'll have to move our stuff out before the authorities shut the whole place down."

Steps of three people hissed against the cool stone of the staircase. "The password for the security system's gotta be up in his place. He'd never leave that down in that excuse of an office." Gina recognized the voice of the man who'd done most of the talking.

"The keys?" The woman.

"Here."

"Wipe them off."

Blood?

"I already have. What do you take me for, an idiot?"

The woman snorted just as Gina retreated back up the staircase. "I believe that's already been established."

"He was your contact, darling." The first man again. Why didn't the second man speak? Was he just a hired gun, the way Peter and Vera had their armed detail?

Their merciless and unstoppable progress drove her up, and now she wished she had clicked the door shut.

The bickering voices approached.

She slipped out to the balcony.

A kingdom for a trellis. Or a fire escape.

She looked down, past the masonry wall. The sheer drop ended on the ancient cobblestones of an alley so narrow, a car couldn't possibly pass through it.

She couldn't go down, but she could go up.

And she did, painfully aware of the chair she'd had to leave under the gutter.

She didn't feel the hot roof under her hands, the grit of terra-cotta tile under her sandaled feet. Just her heartbeat, thudding and painful, and the roar of adrenaline-laced blood in her ears.

The skylight was within reach. She couldn't go in, not this time. It was up for her, up and over the crest of the roof, where she could hang off the other side until she could make her way down to the balcony again.

"Hold it." The man's voice sounded from within.

With a familiar and metallic sound, a gun slide clicked into place.

Then another, and another.

Three guns.

"He'd never leave it open!" The man again.

"You. Go check the outside." The woman.

Gina was screwed. She knew it as she scrambled, as silently as she could, up the roof.

She was above the skylight now.

Heavy steps announced her unwelcome visitor. The other man. Well, she could play cute and stupid. In a way, that's what she was, that's what she felt like.

How could I end up on a roof in Limassol, again?

If she was going to play her femme fatale card, dressed in a tablecloth and an old man's workout shirt, she'd have to ham it up. Sit sideways, show some leg. Quick!

The man who walked onto the terrace looked a bit under six feet, with handsome shoulders and short, brown hair. Gina shifted onto her left hip, working her right leg out to flash some skin. She'd love to straighten her hair – but to that, she'd have to let go with one hand.

The hot roof seared marks into her pale thighs by now, or felt like it did. Into her hands, too.

Letting go with the worn, sore fingertips of her right was a relief. She brushed her hair out of her face just as the tall-and-handsome below turned to survey the porch.

Patio set, a closed umbrella, a chaise lounge. Plants.

Don't look at the roof, don't look at the roof...

He looked at the roof.

Their gazes locked. Gina cramped in her wanna-be femme fatale position, tried to look as though she spent time on hot rooftops for the sheer thrill of it.

And he just stared at her.

"Zhenia?" Gina whispered. "Is that...?"

He gave a minute shake of his head, didn't quite suppress a wry grin, and headed back for the door. "Nothing of interest here," he called out in a native British accent, and to Gina's surprise, he winked at her.

Zhenia, the Ukrainian thug who didn't speak English, cleaned up very nicely with a shave and a haircut. He wore a loose, off-white linen suit, blue shirt, and dark tie. His suit jacket was open, and as he holstered his weapon, Gina didn't see any evidence of his recent injury. That was surprising, but good. The British accent, though. Who did he work for, really?

She stayed still as he disappeared back inside.

Gina didn't know who he was or who he was working for, but he certainly wasn't just an ordinary hired gun. She'd loved to have stayed by the open skylight and listen in, but her legs were getting stiff from their cramped position and her fingers, red and sore, threatened to give out.

Slowly, quietly, letting gravity aid her, she half-slid her way down to the terrace.

Now what?

Staying was a risk.

So was moving down the stairs.

She thought back to Zhenia, injured and broken and in pain. Zhenia who had settled down behind her on a car seat, huddled under coats and bags. He'd squeezed her leg for comfort back then, and she'd helped him eat and drink and get his meds.

Zhenia, who didn't give her away.

Sometimes, life came down to irrational decisions. To trust.

Gina peeked into the stairwell. There he was, Mr. Tall-and-handsome in his sharp looking suit, keeping lookout by the door.

Their gazes met. He jerked his head in a "hurry up" motion. She tiptoed past him.

"Thank you," she mouthed at him, not daring to make a sound.

He winked again.

Gina had never tiptoed down a staircase that fast in her life.

CHAPTER 23

Peter picked up the hotel room phone again, gave the international operator his credit card number, and let it ring. The nine hour time difference between Paris and California was wearing his patience thin and his anxiety over Zeno's radio silence had his stomach flip and twist at every meal.

"Hello?" The voice on the other end was distant, with a faint transoceanic echo marring the reception.

"Aunt Yelena? It's me."

"Ah." He detected satisfaction in her sigh. "You want to talk to you uncle."

A beat of silence.

"Hello." Deeper this time, and a lot shakier than when they last spoke in Vienna.

"Uncle Ilya, it's..."

"I know. Look. Wherever you are, move. Now." The *don't say aloud where you are* subtext was understood by both of them.

"I've moved." No need to broadcast the details.

"*Molodiec.*" There was a smile in that old, "good lad" expression, even though Peter couldn't see the old man.

"How're you doing?" Peter's question had nothing to do with Zeno's radio silence, and an irrational urge to see his uncle gripped his gut. He wanted to be there to see him better, or to see him die. Just this interminable waiting, not knowing how things would pan out – it was grinding Peter into the ground.

178

"Better," Ilya grunted. "The drugs work, but they make me tired. And sick. It's hard to eat anything."

"Have the boys get you some pot," Peter said in a serious voice.

"Um... the stuff stinks like burning catshit, my boy."

Peter forced a laugh. "Good, good."

"I'm not saying I'll try it."

"Of course you won't." Precious seconds ticked by, tallied at an exorbitant rate and charged to Peter's Visa card. "My friend's ignoring me."

"I know. There's nothing you can do about that." A hint of warning seeped through Ilya's voice.

"He can be a stubborn jackass," Peter improvised, thinking of the untold ears that might be listening to a line that was most likely tapped. "I sent someone his way, I hope his lack of manners won't tick her off."

More silent seconds, tense, nervous.

"Oh?"

Peter shrugged, knowing Ilya couldn't possibly see him. "Vera's friend. Ask auntie."

"I will, I will. Well, not much you can do to control someone that far out of your reach." And there was audible reproach in that statement. Peter should've guessed Zeno Lipertis might have had bad company. He just didn't expect the whole situation to go to shit so soon. And if Gina got tangled up in all that, he'd feel doubly responsible.

And nobody expected the war to break out so easily.

Damn.

"If she comes back... "

"If she comes back, have your wife offer any support she can." The subtext here was obvious as well. Don't screw with Gina – and Gina may come back as damaged goods.

It occurred to Peter Ilya must've known something. Something unusual. The line was not secure, though, and this was a lousy time to talk about such things.

"Yes. I'm glad to hear you're doing better. I think we might travel up to Copenhagen. Vera enjoys the symphony."

They'd never go to Denmark, not this time of the year. Tunis, maybe. Or back West. Vera might enjoy a bit of tropical sunshine after this whole ordeal.

"You do that. Give'er my best."

The line went dead. Peter hung up, thinking.

Zeno Lipertis was probably dead. Gina probably hadn't even been there when it happened – her trip must've occurred already. University calendars varied, and as a graduate student who worked in the field, Gina had a lot more latitude than most. She probably would've gone right away – wouldn't she?

He was just being a worrywart.

The hotel hallway floor creaked outside the door.

Peter jumped off the bed, drew his gun, and pressed his back against the wall.

"Just me," he heard Vera say. He stayed where he was. She might not have been alone.

She was.

She had a nylon net shopping bag slung over her left forearm and her hand was on the key. Her right hand was in the right pocket of her blazer. The fact that her gun was at the ready reassured him.

"Oh hi, you're here!" She locked the door behind her, dropped the groceries on the large bed, and holstered her little pistol in the small of her back.

"Yeah," he said on an exhale. "The guy I was supposed to meet didn't show. Zeno isn't answering his phone. If we were at home I'd send him an email, but here..."

"No computer access. I know." What passed for a laptop was as heavy as a small suitcase, and she knew that Peter still didn't trust the Old World phone lines. "Did you call home?"

"Just got off. They say to move along and go somewhere nice. There's nothing I can do."

"Nothing *we* can do," she corrected. "But consider, she's pretty smart. Capable. If she got in trouble, she'd likely get out of it."

"There was nothing in the paper, either," he said. "I checked several."

Vera laughed. "You expect news to appear on the page as though it reported itself! If there were issues, and especially if they found the body of an American student, an attractive woman, you'd hear about it."

"No news is good news," Peter grumbled. "We should've gone to Cyprus as soon as the Bosnian connection became apparent. I should've known he'd become a target."

Vera kicked her low-heeled pumps off and disappeared into the miniscule bathroom. He heard the water run for a bit. Then she came out and pointed to the bed. "Lunch. Come eat."

Paris had a way of distracting a man. The cheeses alone were hard to describe, and the bread crunched delicately, exposing a moist, luscious crumb. Nobody made white bread like they did in Paris.

Some wine would be nice but they made do with bottled water. They had to stay sharp.

"Figs? Clementines?"

He nodded. The vibrant scent of citrus peel infused the air as he dug his nails into one. "Zeno used to love clementines."

"Maybe he still does," Vera retorted.

He just shook his head. "No. I have a bad feeling about this. He just... I..." Peter sipped more water. Then he toyed with the long, curling peel, all thin and orange and temporarily fascinating. "We should've gone there."

"I know," Vera said. "I know. But we couldn't. We had other dates to keep."

Ilya's dates. A stupid lunch with a man named Walt in Munich, who queried him while walking through a river-island park as the bitter, freezing wind cut through their clothes. Walt, whom he didn't know, but who knew Ilya.

Uncle Ilya had told Peter to share information, and Peter did, but he wasn't happy about it. Walt looked like he'd been ridden hard and put away wet. At least he'd had the decency to ask about Uncle Ilya's health. When he'd shaken Peter's hand and informed him it would be a pleasure to do business in the future, Peter's balance shifted. It felt like one of those little earthquakes they got in California every so often, the kind that barely made the local news.

"Uncle Ilya must've known Walt from way back," he commented as he put the mineral water away, wishing it had been something a lot stronger.

"Quite probably."

"I hate this business," Peter hissed. "I hate it with a passion. All I want to do is trade diamonds. I can make a decent living doing that. Hell, better than decent. Why does everyone keep pulling me into their crap, again?"

"Because you're the catalyst." But Vera's expression was tense, and worry lines appeared on her forehead. She'd been like that ever since they'd stowed the artwork in Vienna and gave their own security detail the slip.

He didn't know who, but someone on the team had been an inside man. The ones who had nothing to fear would come back. The one who wouldn't show up was the one he wanted to strangle right now – even though he didn't yet know who he would turn out to be.

CHAPTER 24

THE SHORTER days made for a dark corner in the harbor near the pier. Gina had her ticket for the voyage back. Her berth wouldn't make up for the loss of the luxurious, clean bed in the Limassol hotel she had to leave behind, but its lumpy mattress was worth its weight in gold in security.

Distance from the local police. Escape from the unknown entities who'd killed Peter's contact. Anonymity from Zhenia's British employers – if he kept his pretty mouth shut.

She looked around. Her current situation reminded her of that cold, early December morning in Podgorica. There had been a moment back there and then when Gina came to the unpleasant realization that she was stuck and had very few options open to her, none of them pleasant.

This was different. She had money, transportation, and relative control. So why did it feel so similar? Why did her stomach flip every time she saw a man in uniform? Or in a jacket that might conceal a weapon. Or a radio. Or something... something deadly.

Two hours to go. She considered getting her sketchbook out and drawing the stark, light-and-shadow outlines of the ships moored by the nearby piers. The idea was short-lived.

Bloody handprints.

No, she couldn't pull it out. Not because she was squeamish – she wasn't – but because she didn't want to endanger her hard-won evidence. The dagger she'd prised out of Lipertis' dead body was sharp and pointy, too, and if she jostled the contents of her backpack too much, its sharp point would work its way through the backpack's bottom.

A crowd began to form. Most passengers chose to wait outside, just as she did. The temperature was balmy and the breeze was rushing off the sea, cool and refreshing. She was glad she'd risked a trip to the hotel to retrieve her duffle bag. Aside from freezing, she'd have drawn attention, dressed in just a black workout shirt and a tablecloth.

Jeans and sneakers, a long-sleeve T-shirt and a zippered light jacket. She looked her role now – an American college student on her way back to school.

More people filled the waiting area, filling the benches and the patio chairs, crowding the concrete floor with their luggage. The air smelled of fried fish and garlic and herbs.

Once again, a stranger flicked his or her eyes toward her, just sitting in the dark corner.

Nobody sat in a dark corner.

In her desire to hide, she managed to stick out like a sore thumb. She stood, stretched, and yawned, making a show of how very tired she was after all that fun in the sun.

Others were eating, drinking, talking.

Gina fished her wallet out of her pocket and headed for the local version of a fast-food stand.

Ten minutes later, she was settled on the ground, back against a sturdy fence, a paper tray of stuffed grape leaves and batter-fried fish in her lap. The local Coca-Cola came in very small glass bottles and tasted a little different from what she was used to, but it screamed her allegiance the way her new tourist map in her lap proclaimed her innocence.

The crowd parted. A group of four policemen entered the area.

One of them cleared his throat and said something in Greek. The crowd fell silent. They all looked around, inspecting their fellow passengers. Gina did the same. Other college-age people sat to her right, two German girls and a guy. Over by the table, and old woman dressed in black, a couple with a baby. Tourists, locals, travelers.

One of the police repeated the Greek words in English. "We are looking for a suspicious man. Dark hair, blue eyes, tall." His accented English bore the unmistakable stamp of British instruction. He gave up in his effort to communicate and produced several photocopied black-and-white posters. "He looks like this."

184

Gina craned her neck along with everybody else.

A hand-drawn rendering, most likely by a police artist. White suit, dark shirt, black tie, a conservative haircut. *Zhenia.*

Except Zhenia had been in the front of the store while the murder – or murders - occurred. Nobody else had been in that warehouse – she'd have heard their footsteps. She was sure. One didn't forget moments as fraught with tension as what had happened almost ten hours ago.

She shook her head at the policemen, indicating she hadn't seen a man like that. As soon as his back was turned, she took the poster off the table, folded it, and stuck it in her pocket.

AS SOON as the police left, Gina felt an arm snake around her shoulders. "Hey, babe," he said, sounding as American as she was. He settled on the ground beside her.

She whirled as though stung.

Zhenia.

But not Zhenia, not the way she'd seen him just hours ago. Gone was the civilized suit and tie. The young punk next to her was wearing ripped, paint-splattered jeans and leather construction boots. A gray T-shirt peeked from under his muted plaid flannel shirt, which was barely covered by a thin, leather motorcycle jacket that had seen better days.

He was filthy, his hair was shaved off his head, and he sported three silver hoop earrings in his left ear. She thought a black eye was beginning to develop on his left side, but she couldn't be sure under the dim artificial lights of the pier.

"Hey," she said instead. "Nice of you to show up." That was neutral – wasn't it? She'd return his favor and not blow his cover.

His smile was tinged with relief. He reached into her plate and snagged a piece of food, now cold and nondescript, off her paper plate. "Thanks," he said. "You're a doll!"

Their eyes met. Whoever he was, whatever his real name was, he wasn't thanking her just for a piece of fish.

"You got your ticket?" Curiosity tugged at her. She wanted to know how Zhenia fit into all this. If they ended up traveling together again, she might have an opportunity to find out, as long as she kept her own cards close.

"Yeah, sure." He fished inside his leather jacket and pulled out an old, beat-up American passport with a travel ticket holding his ID page.

She snatched it from his hand.

He let her. His right arm, which he brazenly draped over her shoulder, got heavier.

"I bet your photo's worse than mine," she said, forcing a giggle. To all onlookers, they were just a couple. Or friends. Maybe even classmates.

His photo showed a tight haircut, no jewelry. The name said Eugene Watson. She scanned his home address in Chicago, working hard to memorize it.

"Probably," he said mildly. "Can I have it back now?"

She leafed through the stamps that signified his various ports of call. "You're pretty well traveled for a starving college student."

"Nah," he drew out in a deliberate, lazy way. "I'm a trust fund baby. I can go wherever I want." He grinned. "I took some time off between college and grad school, but I'm still deciding what to do with myself."

"I see." He was feeding her bullshit, but it would do.

For now.

They'd travel on the same boat and then part ways in Sicily. She'd shake the information out of him along the way.

CHAPTER 25

THE ITALIAN boat slept two hundred and was faster than the jumped-up local dinghy Gina sailed in on her way to Cyprus. She was on portside, grasping the white railing hard, looking back as the lights of Limassol shrank into a congregation of fireflies on the horizon, only to recede into the night.

Just as well. Days ago, she'd been excited about Cyprus and its historical treasures. The Orthodox Church connection between Cyprus and Kiev spanned over eight centuries. She'd wanted to see the evidence of this bond in churches, icons, paintings. She'd yearned for adventure, discovering new streets and foods and vistas, meeting new people, forging professional connections.

It took her less than a day to accomplish most of that. No churches, true, but she'd seen more adventure than she'd bargained for. Her new professional contact was dead, but the vista from his sun-scorched rooftop had certainly been one she'd never experienced before.

And, Eugene. Zhenia. She'd never expected to run into him here –nor anywhere else – nor did she expect to meet anyone she already knew. Zhenia was a Russian name equivalent of Eugene. Nothing sinister there, except he had sounded as British as his unseen clients in that big old house, and he'd known to latch onto her and get out of town while his serious face showed up on police posters all over Limassol.

Maybe all over Cyprus. The police could've faxed the image to other cities. Gina didn't know whether Cyprus had any internet

187

connection to speak of. It wasn't like back home, where AOL was in every fifth middle-class household and "having e-mail" had become a higher status symbol than a Coach handbag.

No, maybe they didn't even have a fax machine. Maybe Eugene got out just before the printed copies of his image spread all over the little island.

She frowned into the darkness and shook a stray, wind-blown strand of hair out of her eyes. Zhenia's – Eugene's – presence on this ship was probably not a coincidence.

Maybe he had followed her.

Could be, he wanted to pump her for information as much as she wanted to juice him.

Her cabin was locked and the evidence was still secure in her backpack.

Unless he could pick a lock. Gina knew how, after all, and after what she'd seen in the last two months, she'd never underestimate an enemy.

SHE UNLOCKED her cabin and looked around. Everything seemed in order, her duffle was on the floor by the small fold-down table and chair, her backpack was on the foot of the bed, almost blending with the plain blue blanket.

After she locked the door, she shoved the bathroom door open and peeked in.

Empty.

No one was hiding behind the frosted glass shower door and the space was too cramped to conceal an extra towel, let alone another person.

The cabin was so tiny, two long steps took her to the foot of her bed again. Gina clicked on the small reading light and aimed it at the bed. The pallid overhead light barely good enough for navigating her small space. Now that she wasn't casting constant shadows over her belongings, she proceeded to unload the backpack, methodically, item by item.

Camera. Film. Sketch pad. Pencils. Knife, wrapped in an old map. The workout shirt and tablecloth that had served as a getaway outfit free of drying blood. Few personal toiletries, wallet, keys to her student apartment.

Not being able to use her sketch pad irked her. Hiding the whole big thing was inconvenient, too – and the fingerprinted pages had already been ripped out. Gina folded them in two pages of a complimentary Italian newspaper.

Few headlines caught her eye – she'd read those later. First, wrap the folded, heavy archival quality paper bearing three sets of fingerprints.

She did that, and she used another piece of paper to wrap up her three rolls of spent film. There were two others, but those contained incidental tourist photos from the trip down and over. Now she was glad she had them – they made innocuous decoys.

And the knife. She sacrificed a film canister and three Band-Aids, taped the plastic container over the pointy knife edge, and lined the knife and the film package over the fine art paper she sacrificed to bear witness to bloody death.

The tablecloth she'd used as a wrap-around skirt was still in fair condition, and its embroidery made it look like the sort of a thing a young woman might pickup in the market as a souvenir. Folk art, embroidery... she used it to wrap up her tidy parcel, paying attention to smooth edges and presentation. Like she was making up a gift package for her mother.

Had she been back in the States, a plastic bag would be just a hand's reach away. In Europe, people reused plastic bags. They weren't as ubiquitous, and she had to hunt a bit. There was no handy garbage can liner, no used-up shopping bags, no free bags from stores.

Where was all that waste when she needed it?

Gina lifted the bottom of the mattress and slipped the slim package under it, on top of the steel wire webbing that made up the structure of her bed. It was an obvious hiding place, true, but it was better than her backpack and right now, she couldn't think of anything more secure.

189

She fluffed up the blanket to make it as though someone had rested on the bed, and set her duffel bag by its foot to disguise the uneven slope of her cot. Then she washed her hands, brushed her hair into a new and better ponytail, and set out to the main deck area to grab something small for dinner.

AFTER A DREAMLESS night and a boring day of mingling with other passengers and catching up on the war news from Yugoslavia, Gina ran into Eugene at dinner. He wore the same torn, dirty jeans and plaid flannel shirt as before and his skinhead skull stood out in the crowd.

"May I?" He showed up with a full plate at a table she'd had all to herself so far.

"Sure." She tried to sound casual, but her heart leapt with excitement. This was her big chance. She could gather information. Covertly, of course.

"Were you in Cyprus long?" His quiet baritone surprised her.

She shrugged. "Not long enough to see all I wanted to see." She glanced up from her pasta. "You?"

"Longer than I expected to be."

Evasive non-answers on both ends. This wouldn't get them anywhere. She tried another approach. "How's Vera and Peter?"

He shook his head. "I don't know. We split in Vienna."

"Split? Really? They left you behind?"

He shook his head. "No. They wanted to travel alone."

"But, Zhenia. Don't they need a... a *detail?*" She remembered the casual way in which Vera had waved off the presence of armed guards whose presence had been irritating, but expected.

"Eugene." He corrected her a hard look. "That other guy? He's someone else. You must be mistaken."

She eyed him shrewdly. "Okay." They dug into their buffet dinner. Few minutes passed, enough to assuage hunger, and during this time Gina observed Eugene and his careful, upright posture.

"How's your shoulder?"

190

He stopped in mid-bite, then resumed eating. "Fine." Except it wasn't, not mere four weeks after his accident. A broken bone took six to heal properly. Eugene was taking a risk, acting as though he was all in one piece. She wondered why.

The memory of almost being run off the road flooded in out of nowhere, and on its heels came the image of dark cherry pudding, its streaks smearing a concrete warehouse floor.

"Good." The food seemed too salty all of a sudden and the noise of the dining crowd invaded into their careful, private bubble with a roar, as though she'd been so focused on him, she had tuned them all out.

The dark tomato sauce. Sticky, dark red. Almost like...

She pushed the plate away.

"No good?" He gave her a smirk. "Getting seasick already?"

"No. I don't get seasick." She sipped a bit of pearlescent mineral water out of its green bottle, hoping its fizz and mineral taste would wash the unwelcome images away. "All food's pretty good in these parts."

"Is that why you're all green all of a sudden." He took a big bite, chewed, and swallowed without taking his eyes off her face. "Y'know, we saw what you saw. It wasn't pretty."

"I don't know what you're talking about." Not the most original evasion. She mentally kicked herself.

"We found your footprints in the dust."

She sipped some more. "Who's 'we'?"

He leaned back into his chair and gave her a wry grin. "We could quit dancing around and cut to the chase."

Fresh air had never sounded better. "Upper deck," she said.

Ten minutes later they leaned into the wind at the bow of the ship. "So, tell me, Gina." She felt his elbow brush hers, warmth seeping through her long-sleeve T-shirt. "If that's your name, that is – tell me, how did you come to meet the Christoff's?"

She laughed and leaned in closer, where the sea breeze wouldn't snatch her words away. "You were there – or were you with the cars? I forget. The church in Podgorica, remember?"

Eugene groaned. "So many churches. The woman's a fanatic."

191

"And a good thing, too. Did you know she's highly respected in academic circles?" Gina didn't know where this need to jump to Vera's help came from.

"Academic circles, huh?" His amusement was so obvious, Gina didn't bother looking at Eugene's face. She stared at the white foam caps on the waves instead, fascinated by the way the prow of the ship cut through them, annihilating them somewhere deep underneath.

"Listen, Gina," he said after a while, "you sound like a good kid. Go study your art. Don't mess around with all this."

"All what?" A shiver passed up her back.

Silently, he took off his jacket and draped it over her shoulders. She felt his heat, and the scent of his body was both familiar and welcome. The warmth, the touch of his hand, hiding under a jacket on a cold day – all that reminded her of sharing a seat in the back of an armored sedan with the man that used to be Zhenia and had hair and didn't speak English.

"Thank you," she said, leaning into him. "This brings back memories."

"It does."

"Would you like to go inside? You must be cold."

"In a bit." He draped his arm over her shoulder. "First, we talk. Look, I don't know who you're working for, but you're not in a good place right now. Whatever you're looking for is probably gone. You look new at this, okay? You look new, but you're nice and I don't wanna see you get hurt." The words spilled out, low and warm and full of intent, right next to her ear.

"I'm just a lowly grad student." She thought back, recounting what Eugene was bound to already know. "Peter gave me this guy's name. I'm tracking down some stolen antiquities. Smuggled artifacts. So much gets lost – with the Iron Curtain down, churches and castles get robbed. If those items get found again, they're outside of their cultural context. So much information disapears. Even trivial stuff – all that can be so important."

He squeezed her shoulders. "Okay, okay. So you're a real Vera Christoff wannabe. I get it. You get all fired up over this old crap, just like she does."

192

"It's not just old crap!" She tried to get from under his arm, and failed.

"See?" His chuckle rumbled through her. "All fired up. And that's great, except you're in the wrong place, at the wrong time."

The dusty warehouse came back to that, and the scritch-and-creep of the dying man in the main aisle.

"I know. That's become sort of obvious today."

"Yeah. Lots of people are looking for missing things."

Eugene was about to loosen his arm and let her go when she said, "So you've seen inside the apartment, right? What do you make of all the artwork in there?"

His arm tightened again. "So you did make it inside."

She'd been wearing the dead man's tablecloth when Eugene had seen her on the roof, but she didn't see the need to point that out. "Yeah. I just needed to use the bathroom."

"Why not walk right out? There's a toilet down in the shop!"

And how did he know that? Was Eugene that familiar with the layout? Or had they spent enough time for someone to go looking for the facilities?

"I heard voices! I couldn't possibly just walk out of that warehouse. Think what would it look like!" She let her voice quaver the slightest bit. It didn't take much imagination to recall the gory scene. She allowed the stored-up tension to well up within her, and sniffled.

"Oh come on. You're okay."

She nodded. An art student would cry. It was, after all, horrible.

"You have a handkerchief? A tissue?" Eugene started fussing over her. "I bet you just froze and then panicked! Not that I blame you." He produced a square cotton handkerchief. "Here."

"Th-thank you." She dried her eyes. "I've never seen anything like that in my life."

"So what did you do?"

The footprints in the dust. Showing her every step.

Her breath hitched. "CPR, of course." Her stomach turned at the thought, even though her words were a lie. "But they were so messy. I couldn't have walked out like that, covered in blood!"

193

"Oh, shit." Eugene drew her into a warm embrace, his jacket on one side and his chest on the other. "Lemme guess, you've never seen a dead body before."

She shook her head.

Nor have I ever fingerprinted one. She tried to banish the memory of cooling skin.

"Everything's gonna be okay," he hummed into her hair as they rocked with the ship's increasingly rougher passage. "You'll be fine. I'll make sure of that. Don't worry about a thing."

CHAPTER 26

Gina dodged around a mother pushing a stroller and ducked into an underpass. It cut under the buildings and to the other street, shaded and empty and cool. Only the hollow echo of her footsteps disturbed its silence. She spotted an arched doorway, one that probably led to the apartments upstairs, and ducked in.

The shadows of Messina were deeper here. She tried to still her breath. Her heart was a drum that seemed to have echoed against the arched stone ceiling, bounced off the cobblestones. Her heart would give her away.

She peeked.

No Eugene to the left, no Eugene to the right.

No suspicious strangers with guns or ear pieces – not that she could see. Sunglasses didn't count as suspicious in this climate, though, but two could play their game.

Gina slid her own dark glasses in place. Then she hoisted her duffle bag over her shoulder, adjusted the backpack straps that had loosen during her headlong run, and set out at an easy pace.

Success – she'd given Eugene the slip. Which was no small feat, because ever since their conversation on the boat, Eugene had made himself Gina's self-appointed protector and wouldn't leave her alone. It would've been sweet – except for the minor issue of dead bodies in a deserted warehouse hundreds of miles to the east.

Despite her best efforts, she found she enjoyed his company, and wished she could've pursued their mutual interest beyond the long looks, shared jackets, and the good-night kiss that still tingled on her lips.

That kiss had probably been a mistake.

Old Walt needed the information she'd gathered, though. She wondered what was in those crates and whether the photos of the crate labels would reveal anything. Eugene was involved in running guns or art or something else. Eugene might've been spying on the Christoff's. A bit of chivalry and a few smoldering gazes didn't negate the fact that Eugene was an unknown factor who didn't necessarily have Gina's best interests at heart.

A trust-fund baby. Gina snorted. An unlikely story.

She made it to the ferry two minutes prior to departure, paid, and hid in a thick crowd of travelers all the way to Italy.

The afternoon bus to Naples was crowded and hot. The smell of cumin and naturally fragrant armpits of Cyprus was replaced by mingled scents of cologne that floated on the undercurrent of winter sweat.

At first, Gina was afraid she'd have to fight sleep. The movement of the bus and the vibrations of its wheels, together with the inescapable heat, soothed her frayed nerves. She had scanned the faces around her, but nobody struck her as either familiar or too curious. The rising and falling backdrop of Italian conversation would have lulled her into a sleepy-eyed somnolence she still recalled from her grandmother's kitchen.

The roads saved her. Those, and the crazy Italian drivers. She heard the bus driver up front honk and shout every so often as he made his way through the traffic of smaller towns. The narrow roads twisted and turned, the ocean on the left, even higher hills to the right.

They were sure to die. They were going to run motorbikes off the road. They wouldn't fit into that ancient tunnel – except they did – and the annoying little melodies the Italians used as car horns prodded her into a state of alert vigilance when the bus driver failed to swerve down a dangerous road fast enough.

Once she got off the bus in Naples, Gina was tempted to kneel and kiss the ground. She struck out for the north of the city center instead. The youth hostel she had used with her classmates less than a year ago would still be open.

It was. She grabbed the upper bunk in a common sleeping room, used her luggage as lumpy pillows, and slept like the dead.

Morning came fast, announced by the stirrings of other travelers. Gina washed up, not daring to take a shower while under time pressure. She returned her key and ventured out to find a cafe that would sell her both a small breakfast and a packed travel lunch.

She tried not to look left and right, but as she did one of her covert scans, she noticed a public pay phone.

Gina pulled out a bill and asked for more change. Calling Vienna would be expensive, but letting Walt know she had something had become a critical problem. If she could do so without traveling back to Vienna, so much the better.

She packed her paper-wrapped lunch in her backpack, trying not to think about its proximity to a blood-stained assassin's blade and the gory fingerprints she had thought had been such a good idea at the time. Tipping the waitress an average amount, she rounded up a fistful of change and stuffed it into her jeans' pocket.

A quick diversion into a restroom and a coin for the attendant took care of her needs. Her pit stop served a dual purpose of avoiding the disgusting toilets at the bus station, and being able to slip out of the cafe using the kitchen door.

The door slammed shut behind her. The side door emptied into an underpass with a courtyard to her left and the street she'd been on before to her right.

She turned left, but the courtyard was a dead end full of doorways and garbage cans. So much for her plan of approaching the phone booth from elsewhere. Squaring her shoulders as though she had legitimate business in the building, she walked through the passage quickly, looked up and down the street, then hurried toward the small square and its public telephone booth.

Few minutes and many coins later, the international operator connected her to the US embassy in Vienna.

"Guten Tag."

"Hi, I was wondering if Uncle Walt was in?"

The receptionist switched to English. "Your uncle Walt. And your name, please?"

"Gina. I need to talk to him, it's a family emergency."

"Please hold."

A recording in Italian prompted her to deposit another five hundred liras or end the call. She dug in her pocket and fed the phone. Expensive seconds stretched into minutes. She fed the phone three more times before she heard the click of being connected, a ring on the other side, and Walt's voice booming through the black receiver.

"Walt here. "

"Hi, Uncle Walt!" She had to ham it up, and she knew the phone line could've been tapped. While she'd been waiting, feeding the phone money, she'd been thinking on her approach. It seemed silly, but nothing better occurred to her, and she didn't want to talk about Cyprus and Eugene and the blood in her backpack on the phone. "Sorry to bother you, but the dog, Buster, you gave me few weeks ago? He chewed something up. And the landlady says you have to take it back, so I was wondering... if you could come and talk to her, that would really help." She paused. "Plus it would be so nice to see you again. So much has happened, and it's so exciting! I even took pictures!" She stressed the word 'pictures.'

Walt cleared his voice on the other line. He was about to speak when the now-familiar voice of the recording cut in.

"Wait, I have to feed the phone!" She dropped few more coins into the metal slot. "Sorry. Go ahead."

"Are you at school now?"

"Not this minute." Traveling with a dog wouldn't have worked, so... being vague would do less damage to her cover story. Not that a fictitious dog was all that clever. "Will you visit?"

"Sure," he said with a sigh. "Damn dog was more trouble than I figured on. Be careful, don't get bitten."

AN HOUR later, Gina boarded a bus for Ravenna. Despite her best efforts she dozed off toward the end of the trip, and when she woke up, the darkness outside the bus windows had left her disoriented. She checked her watch. The date seemed to be off – no, wait, she really did spend less than twenty-four hours in Cyprus. The rest of her time off was spent in transit.

Some vacation.

Yet it wasn't all just a holiday. Her mind turned to the new scholarship fund she'd never heard of before. Her stay in Italy was secure until the summer.

She allowed herself a satisfied smile. Old Walt better appreciate what she had to offer.

JUST ONE more block, trudging the mosaic sidewalk. Small cars were parked in every available nook, motorcycles and mopeds were jammed between them. The street ended in a dead-end courtyard with a small traffic turn-around, and an alley protected by a familiar, wrought-iron gate.

Gina had her keys out and ready. The cold metal caught before it clicked open, the way it always did. She slipped through and shut the gate behind her. Then came the first house key and the second house key, which she had to lock from within as per her landlady's instructions. Italians took their security seriously.

Up three flights of stairs. Two more locks to open, and Gina entered her one-room studio with a breath of relief. She dumped her duffle and her backpack on the tile pad by the door, hung her key ring on the hook by the light switch, and clicked in on.

She froze.

The air was scented with just a hint of pipe tobacco.

"Good evening, Gina." Walt rose out of her stuffed reading chair and set his pipe onto her favorite breakfast plate. "Your call was urgent."

"Walt?"

"Nothing like a rowdy dog to lure me in." He gave her a wry smile. "You must be tired – your bus is two hours late."

She shrugged. "Just running on Italian time." Then she frowned. "Did Signora Bianca let you in?"

"No." His face looked less jowly and aged as he smiled. "This old dog can still hunt. But, please. You must be tired. Can I make you a cup of tea? Coffee?"

Gina sucked in some air through her clenched teeth and stomped over to her kitchen corner. She filled the water kettle, plugged it in, and turned it on. That, and a table-top electric burner, was the extent of her kitchen. There was a tiny refrigerator, but had been turned off during her extended absence, and she had not bothered turning it on before she left for Cyprus. Yogurt didn't go bad overnight, after all.

She turned to face him. "You're an impertinent old man! You're invading my space, and I don't appreciate it. There's only tea, instant noodles, and instant soup. There's no milk. I spent countless days at sea, less than one day in Limassol, and I've been fingerprinting dead bodies and running away from suspicious people all along. And then *you*-" she pointed her finger, "you have the nerve to break into my room when all I want is a shower, the food I don't have right now, and ten hours of sleep!"

Old Walt's back was propped against the wall between her reading chair and the door. He didn't move. "You done yet?"

"No," she hissed. "Put up some tea while I shower and change into something clean." She spun on her bare heel, frustrated in her knowledge that it was hard to make a theatrical exit when your pad consisted of one room, a toilet, and a bathroom with a shower stall and a small sink.

She rummaged in her wardrobe for clean clothes and a dry towel. As she shut the door to the bathroom, she overheard Old Walt's quiet chuckle.

"I will not let my blood boil. I will not let my blood boil..." she whispered under her breath as she locked the bathroom door with the ancient skeleton key, stripped, and stepped into the bliss that was hot water.

Diesels exhaust from the boat, cheap wine, old food, the briny stink of the harbor. Limassol and garlic and sticky maroon bloodstains. Warehouse dust, tile roof scrapes and her own ripe sweat – all that swirled down the drain with the water that was just right, banished by the rosemary scent of shampoo and conditioner and lemon soap. She wanted to stay for hours.

Gina sighed in a contentment she knew was short-lived as she turned the water off and made good use of her towel. Minutes later she luxuriated in the feel of fresh underwear and a clean, crisp cotton dress with side pockets big enough for her necessities.

Her hair was a mess. Her comb was outside.

Time to face reality and give Walt what he came for.

"YOUR TEA is ready." Walt's voice greeted her from the reading chair, and just like before, she smelled the fragrance of pipe tobacco.

"Thanks." She sat down on one of two white-painted chairs that came with her small table. This is where she ate and studied and wrote the rough drafts of her papers on an electric typewriter which she seldom bothered to put away.

The familiar scent of tea awakened her hunger, and her stomach growled loud enough for Signora Bianca to hear all the way downstairs. She added more sugar than she usual and stirred it before she set to comb out her wet hair.

"When you're done with that, we could go get dinner," Walt said. "I feel kind of bad intruding, but it's urgent. What did you find?"

She paused. Would it be easier to discuss her finds before eating, or after? Gory images sprung to her mind right away. "Let's talk first. Dinner after."

TEN MINUTES later, the table was cleared of old work, and only the artifacts she considered evidence of sorts were laid out on top of old newspaper. She told her story in a linear fashion, not leaving anything out. Not even getting lost – but there was no snicker from Old Walt, no judgment. He sat, watching, listening, absorbing. Not once did he interrupt her narrative with a question.

Only the bloodstained blade caused Old Walt to raise his eyebrows in surprise.

201

"So I gave him the slip right off the boat," she said, wrapping up with the way she left Eugene in Messina.

Walt cleared his throat, then posed the first of his many questions. "Did you, by any chance, manage to take a picture of this fellow?"

"No." Gina paused. "But wait!" She launched for her jacket and rummaged through her pockets until she found a crumpled piece of paper. "Here."

She didn't expect Old Walt to say anything when she handed him Eugene's wanted poster. She certainly didn't expect him to chuckle. "What?" She leaned forward in curiosity.

"You certainly do make the most interesting friends," Walt finally said. "That was a dangerous thing, what you did at Zeno's house."

"I know. Sorry."

"Good thing he recognized you."

Gina realized she'd been holding her breath. "Who does he work for, you think?"

"Well, the accent might be a bit of a give-away."

"MI6? Like James Bond?" She frowned. "Don't you think that's a bit obvious? The suit and all, I'd figure he was just cultivating a certain image. He's probably just a poser." The thought left her sad inside. She secretly liked the idea of having a British agent as her friend.

"Depends on who was with him. Remember, when you play a role, you play it for someone particular. Like you did on that roof. Or like he had when he'd been with the Christoff's."

Walt's answer wasn't a yes or a no, but it was food for thought.

"I'll take care of the photos. Good job on all this." He produced a soft messenger case from behind her reading chair and started packing her evidence away.

"Will you share the results with me?"

He paused, then looked up and met her eyes with a stern gaze. "Only on a need-to-know basis. The less you know, the less vulnerable you are."

"I'm more vulnerable when I'm kept in the dark." She leafed through her notebook and produced a photograph of Peter Christoff's Serbian letter of passage. "Take this, for instance."

Walt's gray eyebrows rose to where his hairline used to reside many years ago. "Really."

"Yes, really. I was able to translate most of it, and it seems pretty cut and dry. Except for this one little hand-written code on the bottom. What do you make of that?"

He didn't bother taking the proffered photograph from her hand. Instead, he sighed and leaned into the padded back of the reading chair. "You can't know everything. Nobody can. It's a code, yes, but sometimes, you realize something is a kill code only after someone tries to kill you."

She froze. That run at their cars, the way Zhenia got hurt – deliberate, of course, but also predetermined. Who had known to look for the string of numbers and letters? At which checkpoint?

"Are they okay?"

Walt gave her a searching look. "I'm sure I don't know what you mean."

Peter and Vera Christoff and their weapons and bodyguards and artwork. All that. Their generosity and the fishy smell they left behind.

Yet she couldn't say that. He still could be just an arms dealer. A bad guy. But Vera wouldn't be, and if Vera wasn't, then it was hard to believe that Peter, for all his flaws of character, would trade toys with the enemy.

Interrogating Old Walt wasn't any easier in Ravenna than it had been in Vienna. She controlled her sigh as she leaned into the wooden back of the chair and changed the subject. "So what about that knife? No handle on it? Is that also just a need-to-know basis item?" Her tone was neutral, not peevish or frustrated. She was almost proud of herself.

He smiled, once again reminding her of her crazy Uncle Ralph from Hoboken and his moonshine still on top an urban apartment building. "Okay. This I can tell you."

He pulled the weapon out of its improvised sheath, grabbing it through a piece of ripped-off newsprint. "Here, look at the shape, and the tang. And here, if you're careful – " he tilted the blade so the light fell on it just right, "there's this maker's mark. A stamp, see? Almost triangular? That's the Soviet special forces mark. Spetznast, they call it."

Their eyes met.

"But those RPG's came by the crateful," she said. "If you can get so many RPGs for just five Stingers, then it can't be all that hard to get a Soviet knife, right?"

He grinned, happy and wide. "No, no, listen. The Spetznast and the KGB are very close. One recruits from the other. And a knife like this, a blade that flies out of the sheath by releasing a compressed spring, well that's a neat toy, and a guy will hang onto something like that. Blades are very personal. Especially an assassin's weapon designed for close combat situations." He let the cold steel clang onto the table and jabbed his finger toward it. "Gina, this is pretty much a calling card!"

THEY SAT still while the oversweetened tea cooled in Gina's cup. Thoughts chased inside her mind. Concepts overlapped. If this was a KGB knife, and if Eugene was MI6... and all those weapons were being traded even as armies rolled over what used to be Yugoslavia.

She pretty much figured Old Walt was a CIA spook. What she had done – well. She wasn't one of them, but she was part of the larger scene. Part of something big that was taking place under the noses of the ordinary folk who worried about what to make for dinner and how the kids did in school. Her cover access excited her.

Walt sat almost motionless, observing her.

"A proxy war?" She blurted out.

"Yes and no. The Balkans were always complicated. There are definite signs of it, aren't there?" He leaned forward, and his face wasn't impassive anymore. "Would it bother you to be part of something like that?"

Gina thought of Tony and the way he got hurt. If she could prevent some of that, she could certainly justify the risk. Even better, though – this thrill, the elation, the adrenaline of breaking in and climbing on strange rooftops wakened her long-suppressed yearning for adventure. One that she tried to satisfy by doing her graduate research abroad. And now that the research into old antiques turned to smuggling routes, routes that often carried more than just old statues and paintings, Gina heard a new note resonate within. Old Walt's offer had plucked that adventurous string within her soul. She'd find a way to excuse her activities by calling them helpfulness, or just by thinking of herself as another pair of eyes.

Wouldn't she?

"We didn't start the fire," she said.

"Like in that song." He nodded, and packed the rest of his evidence away. "And now, let's go have dinner. I made a reservation at this nice place you'll probably like."

"You did? But how did you know for what time? And why?" She was smiling, though, sailing along with the winds of fate, ready to embrace the next adventure.

Walt shrugged. "Because I'm an impertinent old man."

THE END

Thank you for reading UNSAVORY COMPANY! I hope it transported you to a different time and place!
Please leave a review at a site of your choosing.
Expect to read more about Gina, Vera, and Peter in the future. If you'd like to find out more about my other stories, please use the following Instafreebie link to claim a free Cold War historical short story!
Doing so will sign up you for my newsletter. I promise to write only when I have real news,
and I'll never share your private information:
https://instafreebie.com/free/et961

OTHER TITLES BY KATE PAVELLE

Cancelled Czech Files:

ON THE RUN
NAKED GUN
RAISIN RAID
JUST BLOW IT UP

Honorable Ancestors:
THE RIVER PEARL   *(Heart's Kiss Magazine)*
AIRBORNE FOR LOVE   *(Heart's Kiss Magazine)*
I AM HERE FOR YOU   *(Heart's Kiss Magazine)*

AUTHOR BIO

A prolific writer under another name, **KATE PAVELLE** is a multiple award winning author and an Amazon best-seller. Her novel, *Swordfall*, made the coveted USA TODAY must-read romance list of 2015. Born in Czechoslovakia, she had bummed around Europe as a political refugee before making the USA her preferred home. Kate revels in her rich and joyous family and professional life in Pittsburgh, PA.

www.ingramcontent.com/pod-product-compliance
Lightning Source LLC
Chambersburg PA
CBHW070010260626
47159CB00005B/1744